WALK AWAY

A CHARLIE COBB THRILLER

ROB ASPINALL

MEET CHARLIE COBB

He's known to the criminal underworld as Breaker. The legendary fixer the mob sends in to sort out the scumbags who've stepped out of line.

When he knocks on your door, you'd better be ready to pay up, shape up or get up and run. Only now he's burned his mob bridges. And made some powerful enemies in the process.

Traveling from place to place, he walks the straight and narrow. Yet while the line between good and bad may be narrow, the path to redemption is anything but straight. Because Charlie doesn't have to go looking for trouble. Trouble comes looking for him.

When he sees injustice—rules being broken—he can't help but get involved. And when Charlie's in town, you'd better hope you're on the right side of wrong.

1

The smell of chlorine was strong. The screams of kids splashing around in the pool was noisy. Kim Yunjin stuck a homemade A5 flyer to the noticeboard. She pinned it fast and stood back to read the copy. Doubtless the wording wasn't perfect. With no discernible education, she spoke far better than she wrote in English. Yet the offer was clear. Acupuncture sessions: £40.

Yunjin hoped the advert would work. Local business owners she knew had been kind enough to place flyers inside their shops, pubs and takeaways. She'd also been lucky enough to practice her new skills with free sessions for friends and paid work in Chinatown.

But she wanted to go out on her own. To establish her own business that would provide a more stable income for her and Ji-min. She had spent most of her savings on her acupuncture training, so this had to work.

Yunjin nodded to herself, happy with the flyer. As she walked off along the corridor, she didn't notice the man behind her, tearing the flyer from the wall.

W ith the flyers posted around Hulme and Chinatown, Yunjin walked to the local primary school. It was a mild September day. The afternoon sun warm on her back. Summer had ended and Ji-min had begun her first year in primary school. It had taken more getting used to for Yunjin than her daughter, who loved everything about her new school.

And she was eager to tell her mum about all the exciting things she'd learned as she met her at the gates. Mother and daughter strolled home together, Ji-min in pig tails and a hooded pink coat, with a small rucksack on her back almost as big as her.

They stopped to pick up supplies for Korean pancakes, one of Ji-min's favourites. Plus, seeing as it was Friday, a bag of popcorn for their movie night.

They ate the pancakes at the kitchen table in Yunjin's modest rented apartment. It sat on the first floor of a converted council house.

June, the elderly neighbour below was hard of hearing. She treated Ji-min like a granddaughter. So Yunjin treated June like a grandmother in return, taking her shopping every Monday.

The modest apartment was a vast improvement on some of her previous homes. Yet she wanted somewhere bigger. For Ji-min to have her own room, rather than the two of them having to share a double bed. Not to mention a little outside space where her daughter could play. A more secure environment would be better, too. There had been a spate of break-ins lately, including homeless drug addicts forcing their way into the building.

She had every sympathy for them, but her daughter's safety had to come first.

The acupuncture business would help her move somewhere better. And Yunjin didn't have to wait long for her first customer. At 9am Saturday morning, her phone rang.

It was a pleasant, friendly man called Bill. He'd seen her advert in the leisure centre and was having a problem with a stiff, sore shoulder.

"How soon could you fit me in?" Bill asked.

"You're in luck, I've just had a cancellation," Yunjin replied, pretending to be busy. "How about midday?"

"Oh, you're a lifesaver," Bill said, "I'll see you then."

Yunjin gave Bill her address. She cleaned the apartment and pushed the furniture aside, creating extra space in the living room. Yunjin set up the second-hand treatment table she'd found cheap on eBay and prepared for the session. She tied back her long, black hair and dressed in dark trousers, a white blouse and thin, cream cardigan.

She set Ji-min up in the bedroom with a lunch of sandwiches, crisps, a banana and a juice.

"Mum's got a client coming round, so you'll have to be quiet for an hour," Yunjin said. She handed Ji-min the tablet she used to keep her daughter occupied. "Okay sweetie, what do you want to watch?"

"Frozen!"

"Again?"

Ji-min must have watched the film a thousand times, but if it kept her happy and quiet, who cared? Yunjin plugged a pair of headphones into the tablet and slipped them over Ji-min's ears.

She turned up the volume as Ji-min bit into a sandwich.

"Good girl," Yunjin said, kissing her daughter on the forehead. "Love you."

"Love you, Mum," Ji-min said, eyes glued to the tablet.

Yunjin pulled the bedroom door closed as the intercom buzzed. She checked her appearance in the bathroom mirror. Slim, pretty and very few signs of ageing, even into her late thirties. She picked up the intercom and let the customer into the building.

Yunjin opened the door to the apartment and waited for her very first client. Bill clomped up the brown-carpeted stairs in a pair of black-soled boots and ripped blue jeans. He was six-foot and rangy, wearing a green bomber jacket over a black t-shirt. A bulbous head, bald and greying hair shaved close. His rat-like features showed the wear of his years. Eyes tired and crooked teeth a nicotine-yellow.

But Yunjin wasn't concerned with the man's appearance. Only what she could do to help. And besides, Bill appeared as friendly as he'd sounded on the phone. Smiling and saying hello in a broad Mancunian accent.

Yunjin welcomed him in. He followed her through into the living room.

"I'm in between clinics," Yunjin lied. "I hope you don't mind the temporary arrangement."

"Not at all, love," Bill said, feeling his left shoulder.

"Is that the bad one?" Yunjin asked.

"Yeah," Bill said with a grimace. "Been giving me jip all week."

"Well, let's see what we can do," Yunjin said. "Do you want to remove your jacket?"

Bill slipped out of his coat. He handed it to Yunjin. She hung it on a peg in the hallway and returned to the living room.

"You speak good English for a foreigner," Bill said.

Yunjin thought nothing of the comment. "I've been here

for many years." She laughed. "When I first came, my English was terrible."

"You like it here?" Bill asked.

"I love it," Yunjin said, with her usual beaming smile.

"I bet you do," Bill said, with a snort.

Yunjin thought it a strange thing to say and didn't appreciate his change in tone. Yet she motioned to the treatment table. "Do you want to sit down?"

Bill didn't budge. He looked around the room. "You live alone, eh?"

"Yes," Yunjin said, not wanting to mention Ji-min's presence in the next room. She felt unprofessional enough as it was.

"Good," Bill said, "then we won't be disturbed, will we?"

"Uh, no," Yunjin said, an alarming feeling in her gut. "Take a seat and I'll get the needles."

"No need for that," Bill said, a hand behind his back.

Yunjin hesitated. *"Sorry?"*

Bill pulled a small hunting knife from the waist of his jeans. He grabbed her arm and pulled her towards him, a grip like steel. All sense of humanity disappeared from his dark eyes. *"Scream and I'll cut out your fucking heart, you yellow fucking bitch."*

2

I throw another suitcase on the top of the belt. The last of the lot.

It's a hot day in New York. T-shirt soaked through under a high-vis vest flapping open in a warm, dry wind.

I tie the canopy off on the last trailer and drive the baggage truck back to the depot. I park up and turn down the offer of a cigarette from Mick, one of my workmates.

I grab a cold drink from the water cooler, crush the cup and toss it in the bin. Removing my safety gloves, I peel off the luminous yellow vest and open my locker. I slide out my bag, hook it over a shoulder and wish my new pals on the British Airways baggage team a good weekend.

On the way to the bus stop, I slip on my headphones and listen to an audiobook. It's one of the self-help ones I've been wading through.

I've been trying everything lately. Books, courses, seminars. Anything to learn how to think and act better—like a real person.

Meditation is one of the things I've been trying. It's helped a lot with my condition. No hallucinations in over a month. And I'm pretty chuffed with myself for sticking with it. Though I stop short of doing the *'om'* chanting—makes you look like a right dickhead.

While I listen to a chapter on karma and the law of attraction, I hitch a ride on the staff bus to the bus stop for the Q3. It takes me to my digs in Springfield Gardens. A studio apartment on the second floor.

Grabbing a bag of groceries on the way, I bypass the broken lift and plod up the stairs, tired and sweaty. I stash the groceries in the fridge. The internal light is on the blink again. I give it a slap. It holds. I take a shower in a bath made for a midget, mould creeping up the shower curtain and a handheld shower head. It's like trying to wash an Alsatian in a bucket, water splashing everywhere. But it gets the job done. I dry off and wipe down the floor. Mosey into the living area and microwave a spag-bol ready meal to within an inch of its life.

The TV goes on as I open the second-hand laptop I bought down at a nearby pawn shop.

I'm starting to get myself sorted money-wise now. Got a bag of cash under the dodgy floorboard under the faded Persian rug. But I want to fill another bag before I start investing in new stuff.

Stuff like a bigger place, a car, a phone that gets a signal and a computer that doesn't crash.

I've been working every shift going the past few months. I'm in the best financial shape I've been in for ages. Physically, too. The job has knocked the creeping belly fat into touch. My shoulders are like boulders. And my biceps like bloody rocks.

I reckon I look like I did ten or fifteen years ago. Well, maybe not in the face. But then I was never exactly a GQ model.

Yep, after a summer of throwing heavy cases on the back of trailers, I'm fit as a fiddle. And tanned from the New York sunshine.

I slurp a mouthful of rubber spaghetti and browse the internet. I like to check the news at home. Politics—a waste of everyone's time. Football—new season, same teams winning everything. So I scroll through the local stories on the Manchester Evening News website.

There's a feature about a recent rise in break-ins and gang violence. Some of them related to organised crime. Yeah, no surprise there. now that I'm no longer around to maintain the order.

I suck up a long string of spaghetti and click on a story about a murder. A thirty-eight-year-old woman dead in her apartment. Found by her elderly neighbour. The door to the apartment left open. The woman found on the floor of the living room.

Raped. Murdered. I shake my head. *Terrible.*

I read more on the story. The dead woman has a name . . . I drop the fork. Spaghetti falls from my mouth. I sit on the tiny, battered couch, numb. Utterly fucking numb.

I scan the article again. Make sure I read it right. Make sure I'm not imagining things.

No, I'm not imagining it. That's her name, right there. I pick up a glass and take a drink. My hand shakes. It never shakes.

I feel sick to my guts. The ready meal curdling in my stomach. I stare at her name. Kim Yunjin.

Yunjin. My hand squeezes. The glass explodes.

I shake off the fragments and pick the shards out of my palm.

I Google some more on the story. No motive. No witnesses. No suspects.

I snap the laptop shut, a fire rising in me. I'm up on my feet, pacing the studio.

Hanging's not good enough for the scumbag who did this. And the police can't be trusted to catch the fucker. Their record stinks.

Someone's gotta do something. *But if I go back . . .*

I clean up the mess. The glass. The water. Scrape the remaining spaghetti into the bin. Pour myself a whisky. Two. Three.

Staring at the infomercials on TV, I watch a guy cut through a shoe with a kitchen knife.

As dusk turns to night I decide to sleep on it. For all of ten minutes. I spring out of bed and grab a large black holdall from the top of the wardrobe.

I stuff it full of clothes, move across the floor and shove the coffee table out of the way.

Lifting the corner of the rug, I throw the whole thing aside. I remove the wonky floorboard and pull out the brown grocery bag with my saved up cash.

I take out the stacks of bills and hide them away in the holdall, inside the lining of a coat I don't wear anymore. I had it customised by a cheap, local tailor with a zip up the inside, which makes it perfect for transporting cash through customs and scanners.

I replace the floorboard, flatten the rug and put back the table. Zipping up the holdall, I hook it over a shoulder and leave the apartment.

I stride down the street to the bus stop. The Q3 isn't long in coming. I get on and ride it all the way back to JFK.

3

I board a British Airways 747 from John F. Kennedy to Manchester International Airport. The flight is half-empty, the holidays over. I blagged the job at the airport using a fake name, a made-up CV and falsified documents. The number and email for my reference were real. An old mate at Manchester Airport owed me one. So he was happy to pretend I was on his team.

One of the perks of the job is free air miles and discounted flights. It comes in handy at times like these.

I settle into my window seat behind the left-hand wing having opted for a one-way ticket. A return ticket's no good to a dead man. And the landlord will take care of the apartment should I not make it back and the money stops.

I crack my neck left and right, my knees wedged against the seat in front.

The plane takes off. A night-time flight. We bank over New York. A twinkling neon circuit board pulsing with tiny life.

As the 747 nears cruising altitude, the cabin crew get on with the important business of drinks. Mine's a whiskey taken straight. I knock it back, trying to get the news about Yunjin out of my head. I glance across the cabin. A young couple from the Far East with two young children. Quiet as mice, watching kids films on their headphones.

I close my eyes. But all I see is Yunjin . . . The last time I saw her, and the first time we met.

4

M anchester, 1998

Fucking horrible, this job sometimes.

Not cause of this twat's blood all over my coat. 'Cause it's bouncing down with pissing cold rain.

Doesn't matter whether it's cracking the flags or freezing a brass monkey's bollocks off. If the boss says he wants something doing, he wants it doing. Whatever the fucking weather.

The best you can hope for is the sack of shit you've been sent to sort out settles his debts. That way you don't need to spend long in the alley explaining the gravity of the situation to his front teeth.

I drag Antonio across the yard by his sopping wet mop. His dirty-white trainers kick against the slick, brown cobbles.

I throw him against the back wall of the Italian restaurant, the door to the kitchen shut and the staff keeping out of it. They know the score. But Antonio's a bit slow on the uptake.

The truth is, people will put up with a bit of intimidation from your everyday thug. They say they'll pay, then they don't. They'd rather get roughed up than cough up what's unrightfully theirs.

That's when the boss sends me in.

And if they still don't pay the fuck up . . . Well, everyone has their orders, don't they?

I look at Antonio. His face like a butcher's meat block. He says he doesn't have it. Barely enough breath to breathe, never mind talk. Still, he spits out the words between teeth.

"I don't have any money," he says, eyes rolling, body close to floating in the deep puddle.

"Where have I heard that before?" I say, raising my boot above his head.

But the beeper on my belt goes off.

I lower my foot and check the message. I leave Antonio where he drops and step into the kitchens. There's a phone on the wall. I call the boss's office.

It's the boss who answers.

"Breaker?" He talks in a thick Irish accent. I dunno which part of Ireland. I never asked. "Get your arse down to the clubhouse," he says.

"What for?"

"Never mind what for," the boss says. "I do the whatting for."

"I'm sorting out Antonio."

"He alive?"

"Just about."

"The little shit can wait," the boss says. "Lenny'll pick you up."

I hang up the phone and brush a hand over my shaved black hair, wiping off a layer of rain. I shake the water off my hand and step down into the yard.

Antonio's curled up on the ground, a smack away from dead.

"It's your lucky day," I tell him. "Don't waste it."

I walk through the back gate, hanging off its hinges after I put my foot through it.

I come out onto the street. Lenny's blue Jag pulls up alongside the kerb, driven by Big Joe. Lenny in the front passenger seat, his trainers on the dash.

I get in the back, next to Doughnut Dave. Like sitting next to a talking wardrobe. Joe's not much smaller, dressed in the same black tracksuit. As if they've ever run a mile in their lives. They wouldn't run for a bloody bus.

"Jesus you cunt," Lenny says at me, his mousy hair slicked back as far as the nape of his neck. A pair of thick sideburns and a heroin-thin face and a black leather jacket baggier than an old man's arse.

"What?" I say, as Joe pulls away from the kerb.

"What? You're fucking dripping all over the leather."

"What do you want me to do, stop it raining?"

"No, just beat the cunt inside," Lenny says, lighting a fag.

"It's either this or Antonio's blood," I say.

Lenny shakes his head. "Fucking prick." He slaps Joe on the arm. "Who taught you to drive? Your fucking nan?"

Big Joe puts his foot down. We rush through the pounding rain. I sit cold and soaked to the bone in my own private puddle.

The Clubhouse is an old labour club that sits on its own land round the back of a big estate. It's a flat, brown building with snooker tables and a bar. Plus, a members' lounge and a couple of private rooms with beds for the real business of the place.

The rain has stopped. The jag pulls up outside, alongside a couple of other flash cars.

I get out and follow Lenny, Joe and Dave in through the front entrance. It stinks inside. Blue, beer-soaked carpets and high tar cigs.

There's a click-clack of snooker balls. A couple of old stagers on one of the tables. We march past 'em towards the members' lounge.

I hear the commotion before I see it.

Blood on the carpet and two blokes in suits making threats. One of 'em with his sleeves slashed and his arm dripping red.

Then a girl in the corner from China or Japan or some-fucking-where. She holds tight to a small chopping knife.

I'm pretty sure the only reason that girl is holding the blade and not wearing it in her neck is 'cause members don't dare do anything on club grounds.

It's one of the boss' rules. And you don't break his rules. Not if you like walking on both legs.

The boys in suits aren't armed, either. Shooters left inside cars. Policy of the management.

"Where the fuck is Kev?" Lenny asks of the daytime bouncer.

Steve, the barman tells us he called in sick. "She just grabbed the knife," he says, a half-chopped lime in front of him on the bar.

"And you couldn't stop her?" Lenny asks, eyeballing Steve.

Steve shrugs.

Lenny shakes his head. "You fucking puff." He turns to the girl. "Why don't you drop the knife, sweetheart?"

The girl shakes her head.

"What, don't you sprechen sie fucking English, you kamikaze cunt?"

"Not Japanese, Korean," the girl says, young, pretty, slim. "And you hurt me if I put down."

"We'll hurt you more if you don't drop it," Lenny says. "Choice is yours, love. But you've got three fucking seconds."

"They wanted sex," the girl says, hand trembling on the handle of the knife.

Dave and Joe laugh.

Lenny cracks a smile. "*Er, nurh.* That's what you're here for."

"That's what you're here for," one of the boys in the suits says. "*Stupid slag—*" the guy with the bleeding arm says.

Lenny turns to face him. Gives him a look like he just ran over his grandma. "*You fucking what?*"

The guy falters. "I was just saying."

"I know you were just *saying*," Lenny says, squaring up to him. "Who asked you to say it?"

No answer. Lenny looks over at me. "Get these fuckers out of here."

"We want what we came for," the bleeding guy says.

"And you'll get what's coming to you if you don't watch that fat fucking flap of yours," Lenny says, on the verge of one of his rages. "Now get the fuck out!" he screams in the guy's face, eyes bulging and veins pushing their way out through his skin.

I step in front of him and turn the two members around. I push 'em towards the door. They complain. But not too hard.

"Now my little Chinese takeaway, where were we?" I hear Lenny say on the way out.

I shove the members out of the club and back to their car, a big white Merc.

I see 'em off. Return to the club. Tell the old men to wrap up their game. They drop their cues, neck the ends of their pints, grab their coats and slip out of the door.

I lock the bolt on the front entrance behind them and return to the members' lounge.

Lenny, Joe and Dave are closing in on the girl with the knife,

"Stay back," she says, pointing the sharp end of the blade their way. "I came for hostess job,"

Lenny holds out his hands. "What do you think it meant?"

"Serve drinks, welcome customer," the girl says.

The boys laugh.

"Well sorry sweetheart," Lenny says, finishing a leftover pint. "But our members don't come here for the watered down piss."

He slams the glass down and sighs.

The girl looks from eye to eye. "Then I go," she says. "My mistake."

Lenny takes a step towards her. "Oh, no, no, no. We can't have that. You're a member of staff now. One of the team."

"I don't want pay," the girl says.

"Good, 'cause you're not gonna get it," Lenny replies.

"I don't understand," the girl says, keeping Lenny at bay with the knife.

He dances up and down, pulling on his eyelids. "Oh, sorry mis'er. I doh un'erstan."

Joe and Dave laugh like drains. I stand and watch.

"The only thing you need to understand is that you're our property now ..." Lenny pauses. "*My* property."

The girl seems even more confused.

"Look, sweetheart, let me make this real fucking simple for you," Lenny prowls the carpet. "If a member wants to stick his dick down your throat, you ask how far. If a member wants to fuck you in the arse, you ask what with. You live in a house with the other girls. And you don't get a fucking choice." Lenny puts his hands together like he's praying. "Now," he says, softening his voice, "if you play nice, do a good job and grow some fucking manners, maybe we can see about some pocket money. In the meantime, could you please, please, please, *drop the fucking knife!*"

Lenny screams so loud, the girl drops her guard. The little scrote moves in fast, a hand on her wrist. Dave and Joe in there too. They wrestle the knife from her grip.

The girl kicks and punches. Gotta give her credit, she's got plenty of fight.

But Dave backhands her. She falls to the floor. Staggers upright with a hand to her cheek.

I take a step forward and look at Lenny.

He shrugs at me. *"What?"*

"The other girls wanna do it. Since when did we do slavery?"

Lenny turns and snarls at me. "Since I decided. Got a problem with that?"

Me and the girl make eye contact. She looks at me as if I'm her last hope, not realising who I am. Or what I do for a living.

Lenny stares at me some more. I look away. The guy's a weasel. But there's a pecking order. And he's got a bigger beak.

For starters, he's a blood relative within the organisation. The boss' nephew.

Which means he's got a licence for that arsehole he calls a mouth.

"So," he says, removing his jacket, revealing his scrawny,

wiry frame. "Best give you an audition. Check you're up to the job."

Lenny throws his jacket over the back of a chair. He moves in on the girl. She backs away. Dave and Joe grab her and pull her towards Lenny.

The girl struggles some more and makes eye contact with me again.

Lenny unbuckles his belt. "We'll do her in one of the rooms. I get first dibs."

It doesn't sit well with me. Not in the bloody slightest. It isn't right. But it's not my place. Not like I can do anything.

Well, I could . . . I could do a lot of things. But there are rules. Consequences.

So why am I even thinking it? Just turn around, Charlie. Go and have a game of snooker. It'll be over soon. And she'll live.

Lenny and the lads force the girl towards one of the two doors marked private to the left of the room. They open the door and push her inside.

"You not having a go?" Dave asks me.

The girl screams, Joe holding her face-down on the bed inside the room. I shake my head.

"Fucking queer," Lenny says, unzipping his pants.

Dave throws the door shut behind them.

I turn and walk into the snooker room. The old timers left halfway through a game. Might as well clear the table.

I pick up a cue and line up a shot, listening to the girl's muffled screams.

Like I said, it's not my place.

The shuttle van drops me off at the rental place. I pay for my hire car and drive away from the airport in a brown Peugeot 2008.

This is Britain. So you pay for something with a bit of oomph and they give you one of those family crossovers. Good for ferrying kids around, but when am I gonna be doing that?

Yep, I get the distinct impression I'm being stiffed. Serves me right for hiring through the cheap place. So I swallow my medicine and take the M56 motorway towards Manchester.

The city sits under an autumn duvet of grey clouds. It's ten degrees cooler than New York and everything seems smaller than it used to, not least the city skyline.

Today, I'm headed for a part of the world called Hulme. It's off a dual carriageway that plugs direct into the heart of Manchester. 'Princess Parkway' it's called. Not that there's anything regal about boarded-up shops and broken-down council flats.

But first I'm taking a small detour. I take the road into

the outskirts of the city and pull down a side street between warehouse buildings.

There's a silver Mondeo waiting for me. An old contact from the force.

You can spot a plain-clothes copper a mile off. Especially an unmarked pool car.

I flash my lights three times before I pull up alongside the Mondeo. D.I. Jones winds down his window as I pull alongside. I wind down mine.

He's bald nowadays, with a silver goatee and eyes that haven't seen a minute's peace. Probably the two ex-wives and all the child support he has to pay for.

I hand him an envelope of cash. He peeps inside, runs a thumb over the wad of notes and tucks the money in his coat.

He hands me a brown folder tied with string at the front. We don't even nod. Just wind up our windows and drive in opposite directions.

At the end of the street, I turn the hire car round and head back to Hulme. I pass the brewery, then make a right before the retail park.

After more than a year of moving from one strange place to another, I'm back in familiar territory. And the place hasn't changed at all.

From the news reports on the internet, I'm pretty sure I can find the place I'm looking for. So I drive around for a bit. Past a school, a job centre and a clinic.

Hulme was one of the first places they regenerated to try and improve the areas on the fringes of the city. It's full of low-rise flats and dinky little houses crammed together. There's a college now, too.

Still not the best area, but the place used to be a total dive. I should know, it used to be one of my old stomping grounds back in the day. Druggies, dealers and gangs on every corner.

Yep, I kicked a lot of things in around here. Doors, heads, teeth . . . Ah, this is the place. It's easy to spot. Yellow police tape hanging loose off the door frame. CSI teams long gone. Another open case to add to the pile.

I park the Peugeot on the kerb and stretch my aching legs. I didn't get much sleep on the flight. And those plane seats aren't designed for my six and a half feet.

I open the boot and reach inside my holdall. I dig around and find what I'm looking for. Locking the car behind me, I approach the entrance to the flats. I check over both shoulders and insert the skeleton key into the door.

To the untrained eye, skeleton key tools look a lot like screwdrivers. They don't cost much and you can pick 'em up off Amazon these days.

The lock clicks open. I step inside the door and close it as quiet as I can. I creep up the stairs to the first floor. Find a door with the yellow tape still in place. A criss-cross barring entry. Well, a little police tape never bothered me. I press on the door. It swings open. I lift the tape and duck under it.

I'm inside. The flat is gloomy. Boxy. There's a strong chemical smell. It lingers from the likes of fluorescein, iodine, cyanoacrylate, silver nitrate and ninhydrin. All the tools of the trade to take fingerprints and detect blood stains unseen to the eye.

There's a small, basic kitchen to my left. A two-seater table and less wriggle room than a straitjacket. The bathroom is the same. No signs of struggle in either one. But the living room is different. Much different.

It takes a lot to knock me sick, but the sight of the room does it. Lampshades are knocked over, a glass vase smashed, a coffee table broken and a treatment table overturned.

The carpet is a mess of deep red stains. There are streaks and spatter marks up and down the matte-white walls.

A long, thick trail of blood suggests a body crawling across the room. Or dragged, I can't tell.

I open the police file from D.I. Jones and consult the notes. She was crawling. But away from who?

Fingerprints haven't come up with anything to say who the murderer might be.

I move over to the spot where Yunjin's body was found. A black taped outline of where she last fell.

I consult the photograph of the body. A corpse without a head.

They found the head in the kitchen bin, since taken away for forensics.

The killer used a carving knife from a kitchen drawer.

Which if you've ever had to cut a head from a neck . . . Well, you'll know he must have been here awhile.

The neighbour downstairs heard nothing. She's an elderly woman hard of hearing. Cataracts too. The report says she didn't see a bean.

I continue on through the report, trying to ignore the sick feeling in the pit of my stomach. Trying to keep it together. To keep a clear head.

The report mentions a daughter. No sign of her here. It's unconfirmed whether the case extends to an abduction. My first thought is that it's the dad. But the father's identity is unknown. Unlikely in that case.

I scan the scene again and compare it to the report. I move into the bedroom. It's untouched. The biggest sign of a disturbance a ruffled pink duvet cover.

I lift the duvet and check the sheets for stains. No, the attack was limited to the living room.

But it seems so frenzied. How can he have not left a

fingerprint? He's got to have moved around the flat. And he's sure to have been covered in blood.

I check the report again. No footprints. No hairs. No trace. It takes skill to do that.

So he's got to have done this kind of thing before. A serial killer? Contractor? Mafia hitman?

Was Yunjin into something? Drugs? Gambling? Debt?

Surely not. She wasn't the type. And this wasn't a contract killing. Far too messy.

I check the timings.

Thank Christ for that. He cut her head off after she died.

But he did have sex with her before he killed her. And after, too.

Traces of semen were found on the treatment table, the sofa and carpet. Maybe that's why he moved the body. So he interfered with her body after she died.

As I near the end of the report, I think I hear something. A scratching sound? Probably a mouse in the walls.

I return to the living room. Stand over the largest blood stain of the lot. A circular bleed the size of a lounge rug. This is where she died. A fatal stab wound to the abdomen.

Before that, a severe beating. Jaw broken. An eye socket too. Swelling, bruising and bleeding all over.

Clearly she fought for her own life . . . And her daughter's?

The autopsy shows a man's skin and blood beneath her broken nails. Blood type O-Negative. Someone else's.

It's not enough to go off. But the killer should be sporting some injuries of his own.

I look around, close the report and wander into the kitchen, a little dizzy, a little weak.

There are photos stuck to the fridge with alphabet

magnets. Yunjin and her little girl. Smiles bigger than the moon.

And one of Yunjin on her own, posing on the beach. A blue duffel coat, strands of her own long, dark hair blowing into her face.

The photo knocks the wind out of me. Part of me doesn't want to look.

I pluck it from the fridge anyway, fall back into a kitchen chair and stare at the print.

It's from when she was young. It can't of been much later than . . . Shit, what year was it again?

6

Manchester, 1998

I slam a red into a corner pocket. Chalk the tip of the cue. Get down and line up a shot on the black. But there's no blocking out those screams.

I stand up. Shake my head and bend down low again, cue tip to cue ball. I draw back my arm and whack the ball with the cue.

The white comes clean off the table and smashes an empty pint glass off a bar table.

I turn and stride out of the snooker room, cue still in hand. Walking across the members' lounge, I unscrew the end of the cue.

Steve the barman is polishing a glass. He pauses.

I stop and turn to him. *"Get out."*

He ditches the glass and hurries out through a staff door. I toss the thin end of the cue and continue on my way to the private rooms.

Coming up to the first door, I don't break my stride. I fling the door open.

The girl is stripped to her skirt, bra and shoes, her

knickers round her knees. Lenny tries to force himself on her as Joe and Dave try to keep her from squirming.

I stand inside the doorway. Fat end of the cue upside down. Knuckles squeezing white.

"Let her go," I say.

Lenny freezes, confused. "What's all this shit?"

"I'm relieving you of your command," I say.

He laughs and waves me away. "Daft twat. Get the fuck out of here."

I don't budge an inch.

"You know the rules," Lenny says. "You take another step and you're a dead cunt walking."

Lenny sighs. "Sort this cunt out," he says to Joe and Dave.

They hesitate. Share a nervous glance. They don't want any of it.

"I said sort . . . the cunt . . . out!"

Joe and Dave psyche 'emselves up. They come at me like a tag team, leaving Lenny to wrestle with the girl.

I meet 'em halfway across the floor. A swing and a miss from Dave. I slam the cue-end in his ribs. A backhand swipe splits his nose.

Joe runs me against a wall, a line-backer sacking a quarterback.

I crack him in the spine with the cue. Stick my fingers up his nostrils and push him backwards. I raise the cue to do some damage. But Joe rips it from my hand. He tosses it away. Takes another swing.

Yeah, he's big, but slow. I'm ducking under and inside. Rabbit punches to the gut. A rising head-butt.

Yet Dave's on my back. I'm caught in a headlock. I kick out and boot Joe into a glass cabinet. I grab the top of Dave's head and press the back of my skull into his windpipe.

He coughs and wheezes, letting go. Staggers back. I launch right into him. A right. A left. A one-two combo.

He's wobbling. I grab him by the collar, swing him round and drive his head through the plasterboard wall. I pull his head back out and he drops to the floor.

I stand over Dave. I've known him for five years, but once you get me going . . . I stomp on his throat and it kills him.

I move onto Joe, Lenny struggling to contain the girl. She wrestles, claws and pulls his greasy mop.

Joe hauls himself out of the glass cabinet, cut half to shit. I go to finish him off. He scoops me up over his shoulders and throws me against the wall.

I bounce off and stride towards him. I sidestep the fat bastard and pick up the cue-end. I hit him hard on the back of the skull.

He's down on all fours. I hit him again. He rolls over. I slam the cue-end into his face over and over. Until his jawbone shatters. Until his face is mush. Until my right arm drips with his blood.

That's when I realise Lenny is running towards the window. He has it halfway up. His body halfway out.

I chase after him and grab him by the belt. But his baggy jeans slip off his waist. His chicken legs kick their way out, down to a pair of pink boxers, he slips out of the window. Lands face-first on the grass outside.

As he sprints off, I push the window all the way up and vault out onto the grass. I'm after him, but he's like a rat up a drainpipe. He's in the Jag before I know it.

I give chase, but the Jag has the keys in the ignition. A bad habit of Joe's. Lenny speeds away, tyres skidding and gravel kicking up in my face.

I return to the window and climb back inside. The girl lies on the bed. In shock and fear. In fear of me.

I approach the bed. She tenses up. I pick up her sweater off the floor and offer it to her. She doesn't budge. I motion for her to take it.

The girl takes it. Slips it on. Pulls her knickers back up and slides off the bed.

She gets to her feet. "Uh, thank you," she says, looking at the dead bodies on the floor. She sways as if she's gonna faint. I steady her. She holds onto my arm.

"What—What now?" she asks.

"I didn't think that far," I say.

"Why—Why you help me?"

"Come on," I say, leading her through the mess. "There'll be more of 'em here soon."

7

I 'm sitting staring at the photo when I hear a noise inside the flat. It sounds like a door sliding open. And the pad of feet across carpet.

I'm shocked to see a young girl appear in the kitchen. No more than five or six. Her jet-black hair in a bowl-shaped bob. Chubby cheeks, yet to lose their puppy fat. And big, innocent eyes like one of those Pokémon characters. She's dressed in pink pyjamas, clutching a black and white cuddly cow toy to her chest.

The girl heads straight for the fridge, not even noticing me. She gets a bowl from a knee-high cupboard. A cereal box from another.

The girl pours herself a bowl of Cheerios and opens the fridge. Takes out an open carton of milk and splashes some over the cereal, spilling some on the worktop.

The girl returns the milk to the fridge, stands on her tiptoes and grabs a spoon off the drainer.

She carries her bowl to the table, climbs onto the chair across from me and spoons a mouthful

Milk drips from her chin. She stops chewing and looks

at me. I wait for her to react. To scream. To say something. But she carries on chewing, showing me the contents.

The young girl spoons in the next mouthful. She looks a lot like the girl in the photos stuck to the fridge.

A year older maybe, but it's got to be Yunjin's missing daughter. I knew Yunjin had one. The last time we spoke, she mentioned the girl was three, with a genius IQ for her age. But I'm ashamed to say I never saw her. Never visited. Can't even remember the girl's name.

I shake my head, ashamed. I should have made more of an effort to stay in closer touch. But that's life. You get busy with all the unimportant shit.

I lean forward in my chair. *"Alright?"*

The girl ignores me and chomps through more of her cereal.

"What's your name?" I ask.

She stops chewing. "Ji-min," she says, a gob full of mushy brown Cheerios. "Are you a friend of Mum's?"

"Yes," I say. "Well, I *was*."

"Mum's not here," Ji-min continues.

"Oh?"

"She's in heaven now."

I shift in my chair, almost floored by the comment. "What makes you say that?"

Ji-min digs her spoon in her bowl and hovels some more cereal in. There's a redness around her eyes from where she's been crying. Yet otherwise, the girl seems ridiculously calm. Like it's not really sunk in yet, or she isn't quite old enough to understand what death means—or what it means for her. That she's never going to see her mum again. I was only seven when I found my mum on the living room floor—a needle stuck in her arm and foam round her mouth. I knew what had happened, but the magnitude of it didn't sink in for weeks. Maybe that's what's happening here.

I decide to tread carefully. "Did you see what happened to your mum?"

Ji-min shakes her head.

"Did you hear anything?

She shakes her head again.

I breathe a sigh of relief. "Then how do you know she's in heaven?"

"The police came," Ji-min says, sad eyes staring into sugary milk. "They said Mum was dead. And when people die, they go to heaven."

Now, I'm not an emotional guy. I don't shit my pants during horror films or get excited during the football. And I've never been one of the wobbling-lip brigade.

But I have to admit, I'm not a million miles from a tearful eye.

It's not only the situation. It's the girl's face, like a baby deer.

"How come the police didn't find you?" I ask.

Ji-min puts down her spoon and picks up her stuffed cow. She whispers with the cow in what I guess is Korean. The cow whispers back.

Ji-min slides off her chair. "I'll show you," she says, the cow nodding in agreement. "But Mr Moo says you've got to promise not to tell."

"*Mr Moo?*"

Ji-min launches an arm forward, cow in hand. "Mr Moo."

"Okay," I say, standing out of my chair. "I cross my heart."

"And hope to die?" Ji-min asks.

I nod. "Stick a needle in my eye."

The cow and Ji-min confer.

Ji-min nods. "Mr Moo says okay." She turns and leads the way. We cross the living room floor. She stops and points at the bloodstains. "Do you know what these are?"

"Yeah, wine stains."

"Mum doesn't drink wine."

"Then it's probably juice."

"Oh," Ji-min says, buying it and continuing on her way.

I follow close behind, into the bedroom. She stops and points at the wardrobe. One of those built-in sliding ones. I take a look inside. It's stuffed with hanging clothes.

"You were hiding in here?" I ask.

"Further in," Ji-min says.

I push the clothes aside on the rail. There's a white panel. It looks like the wardrobe ends there, but a little push and it opens inwards. I stick my head round the corner. There's crawl space big enough for a child. A big yellow cushion for a mattress, a pillow and a blanket. There are snack wrappers and an empty water bottle. Plus, a couple more stuffed toys and a tablet with a pair of children's headphones plugged in.

My guess is whoever lived in the flat before Yunjin had a stash of something they liked to keep hidden. Drugs. Guns. Cash. Porn. Whatever the case, Yunjin turned it into some kind of secret den for her daughter.

"You were hiding away all this time?" I ask Ji-min.

"Uh-huh."

"And the police didn't find you?"

She shakes her head.

"Why didn't you come out?"

"Mum says when I go in the secret place, not to come out for anyone."

"Why were you hiding in the first place?"

"Mum shouted the secret word," Ji-min says. "When she shouts the secret word, I hide in the secret place. We practiced a lot."

"In case of what?"

"In case robbers came around," Ji-min says. "Mum worries sometimes."

"But surely it's okay to come out for the police."

"Mum says not to come out until she says. I held onto my wee as long as I could. When I came out, everyone was gone. And the phone was broken."

I point at the crawl space. "So all this time, you've been in here?"

Ji-min holds Mr Moo tight to her chin and stares at the floor. "I don't know where school is and I was waiting for Mum's angel to come." She looks up at me. "I want to be here when she gets here."

I put a hand to my face. Fuck, how do I break it to her that her mum's never coming back?

I don't. *Can't.* It needs someone smarter than me. Better with kids at the very least.

I need to get Ji-min to someone who can help her. Drop her off with the cops, maybe. But that'll get messy. And take time.

Time enough for the scent to get cold. One way or another, I'm gonna get noticed.

"Alright," I say, "let's get your things together."

Ji-min shakes her head. "I need to stay, in case Mum comes back."

I kneel down and look her in the eye. "Wherever you are, she'll find you."

Ji-min fixes me with her big, wet eyes. *"Really?"*

"Of course," I say. "That's what angels do."

"Okay. But can I take all my toys?"

"You can take three," I say. "So choose wisely."

As Ji-min ip-dips from a bunch of stuffed animals, I look for a bag to stuff some clothes in.

The place is giving me the creeps. The chemicals leaving me queasy. The sooner we get out of here, the better.

8

W e pull up outside the cop shop.

"What are we doing?" Ji-min asks, sat on top of my holdall on the backseat of the Peugeot—belt tucked under an armpit.

"Gonna drop you off with the police," I say. "They'll take good care of you."

Ji-min shakes her head. "No."

I turn in my seat. "What do you mean, no?"

"I don't want to."

"It's the only option. You'll be safe there."

"I don't know them," Ji-min says. "Mum says never talk to strangers."

"*I'm* a stranger," I say.

"No you're not," Ji-min says, as if I'm talking bollocks. "You're my uncle."

"Your what?"

"Uncle Charlie."

"How do you know my name?"

"I've seen your picture in Mum's albums. She said your name is Charlie and you're her favourite uncle."

"Really? She said that?"

"You look a lot older," Ji-min says.

"Oh, thanks."

"But I recognise you now," Ji-min says.

"You *do* know what an uncle is, right?"

"Yes, an uncle is someone who is like a big brother. But really, really old."

Cheeky bloody—I bite my tongue. "Well, uncle or no uncle, you can't stay with me."

Ji-min shakes her head. "Families have to look after each other. I need to look after you now."

"I'm sure I'll be okay," I say, ejecting my seatbelt. I climb out of the Peugeot, leaving the engine running. My plan is to dump and run. As soon as I push her through the front door, I'm off.

I open the rear passenger door and go to unfasten the seatbelt.

"No!" she yells. "No police!"

"It's only for a short time," I say. "They'll find you a new home. A new family."

I almost choke on the words. The care system is like the inside of a cow's behind . . . It ain't pretty.

"I don't want a new family," Ji-min says. "I want Mum."

I don't know what to say to her, so I eject her seatbelt and try and pull her off the holdall.

"Let me go!" she yells, kicking and fighting.

"It's for your own good," I say. "Pipe down."

Ji-min screams at the top of her lungs. *"Help, he's attacking me!"*

It's shrill enough to alert dogs on the other side of the city. I look around. People are watching on. I put a hand over her mouth. She shuts up.

"You're gonna get me in trouble," I say. "Do you want that?"

She shakes her head, only her eyes visible above my hand.

"Well okay then,"

I remove my hand. She screams some more.

"Alright, alright," I say, hand back over her mouth. "Will you do it for an ice cream?"

Ji-min nods.

I take my hand away, with caution.

"Two ice creams," she says.

"One with a double scoop," I say, offering her my hand. "Deal?"

"Deal," Ji-min says.

We shake on it.

"But after that, I'm handing you over."

"Okay," Ji-min says, as if she's forgotten why she was arguing.

J i-min gets two scoops like I promised. Strawberry and chocolate with all the toppings old Mario can throw at her. She sits on one of the red leather high stools, kicking her legs in anticipation. Eyes as big as the moon, staring at the rainbow of sprinkles on top of her ice cream. She'd better not puke in the car.

Mario's is a small gelato place that does the best ice cream you'll find anywhere outside Naples. I once sorted a problem for the guy. He was being given a hard time by a pair of local drug dealers trying to move into the protection racket. They picked the wrong day to hassle the small, old Italian man. I was here cooling down on a hot summer day.

A mint-choc-chip in hand. I dunno what those dealers are doing now, but ten quid says it involves a limp.

Needless to say the ice cream is free. But I insist on paying. Slipping him an extra twenty for some information.

"Where does Honest Ed hang around these days?" I ask.

"Down at the snooker club," Mario says, sticking a plastic spoon in Ji-min's tub of ice cream.

"That place still going?"

"Still going," Mario says. "Still full of snakes. Why do you ask?"

"Got some business."

"I heard you quit the business," Mario says.

"Personal business," I reply.

Mario hands over the ice cream. "You're better off out," he says. "It's not like it used to be. People are crazy nowadays."

"You worry too much."

"You don't worry enough," Mario says, like a concerned father. "Just be careful out there."

"Always am."

Mario leans across the counter, curious. "And who's the girl?"

"Oh, she's my niece."

I can see the old man trying to work out the logistics in his head.

I pass the ice cream to Ji-min and lift her off the stool. We wave goodbye to Mario as we leave.

The Clubhouse. Nowadays a snooker and pool hall with satellite TV, dartboards and poker tables out back. A den for lowlifes. The cheap beer and a chance to smoke indoors a magnet for scum. After all, it's not like the anti-smoking police are venturing round here anytime soon.

Anyone who's no one knows *Triangles Snooker and Pool Club*. Not just a place to hustle and gamble, but to get information too.

For some reason, it's one of those dives where the city's criminal underbelly gets talkative. And if there's anything a con likes more than making fast money, it's bragging about what they know, who they know and what they've done.

"Okay," I say to Ji-min. "Back in a jiffy. In the meantime, don't go anywhere. And if anyone comes up to the car. Don't unlock it. Understand?"

Ji-min nods, halfway through her ice cream. Wearing most of it around her mouth.

I get out of the car and lock the doors. I head inside the club.

There's an old battle-axe on reception. Her name's Vera. Short, white hair and forearms that could bend steel. She does her puzzles, looks up and doesn't seem surprised to see me.

That's Vera.

Giant blue aliens could waltz through the door and she wouldn't bat an eyelid.

She taps on the glass. *£5 entry.* I slip her a crumpled fiver.

"Snooker, pool or summat else?" she says, locking the cash away in a red safe box.

"Summat else," I say, striding off.

I push through the doors to the snooker hall.

The place is busy as usual. Some blokes ducking the law, some ducking their wives, others ducking their lives.

A shelf of cigarette smoke hovers at eye level. The gloom interrupted by lights above tables. No one notices me at first. I slip inside and hug the wall, looking for Honest Ed.

The name's ironic. And there he is. A half mullet. His blonde hair greying out. Grey joggers and trainers with an England football shirt from Italia '90.

He lines up a shot, fag in mouth, playing an old man in coke-bottle glasses. A safe-cracking relic from the seventies called Posh John.

Posh 'cause he comes from Cheshire.

As I move across the room, people start to notice. Shots paused. Shots missed. Games interrupted. Pints are supped fast and nervous glances exchanged.

I walk through the tables.

Honest Ed stands on the far side of the hall. I weave through the tables, not knowing what to make of the hush in the room. Are they hostile or plain scared?

Either way, they'll be on their phones the second I'm out of here, spreading the word. So I'd better make this quick.

Honest Ed is the last to notice me. He misses a shot. Curses his own ineptness, stands up from the table and follows Posh John's stare as far as me.

Ed takes the fag from his mouth and breaks into a smile. "Breaker, as I live and fucking breathe."

"Ed . . . John," I say, looking around me, the snooker hall in silence as everyone stands gawping. "Anyone got a problem?" I ask.

There's a moment silence, the tension thick.

After a few seconds more, the clientele return to their games, the room filling with the click of balls and raucous chatter.

Ed nods towards the table. "Fancy a game?"

"Thanks, but I'm not staying."

"Then what can I do for you?" Ed asks.

"What do you think?"

Ed takes a drag of his cigarette. "I think you've been away too long," Ed says, his teeth brown and the years of drink turning his face ruby-red. "I'm not in the information business anymore."

Ed bends down and misses an easy shot.

"Then what are you doing here?" I say. "You still can't pot for shit."

"Well John's blind as a bat," Ed says. "So it evens things out."

"The murder in Hulme," I say. "what do you know about it?"

"What murder in Hulme?"

"The young woman," I say. "You know the one."

"Oh, the chink bird who got her head cut off?" Ed says, sipping on a pint. "Yeah saw it on the paper. Nasty as fuck. The pigs don't have a clue. But when did they ever?"

I stroll around the table, running a finger over the balding felt on the cushion. "Funny, didn't know you could read."

"Posh John read it to me," Ed says.

"Thought you said he was blind."

Ed drinks more of his pint. Smokes his fag a little faster. He's had a few, which makes this easier.

"What happened to you, Ed?" I ask, taking out my wallet. "Used to be a rat couldn't fart without you knowing about it. You losing your touch?"

Ed takes the bait. "I didn't say I didn't know nothing."

I take out a twenty and slip it in Ed's hand.

Ed sighs. "Course, inflation keeps going up."

I give him another twenty. "That's all I've got."

"That wallet looks pretty fat to me," Ed says.

I tuck my wallet away. "I need the rest for the next dickhead."

Ed stubs out his cig and glances over a shoulder. "I've heard a few whispers."

"Whispers?"

"A guy's been talking. Bragging about something he did. Involved a knife and a head."

"This man have a name?"

Ed stares into space. Lets out a big sigh. "A name, a name —What was his name again, John?"

"Don't remember," Posh John says.

"No, me neither," Ed says. "Sorry, pal."

I take out my wallet again and hand over an extra tenner.

"Yeah, it's coming back to me," Ed says. "Yeah, that's him —Bill Duffy."

"Wild Bill? You sure about that?"

"Yep, yep I'm sure."

"Alright then," I say, "Know where I can find him?"

Ed shakes his head. "He's been lying low."

"Lying low where?"

"What am I, his ball and chain? I know he hangs around O'Malley's. You know it?"

"I know *of* it," I say, making to leave. "Nice catching up with you, Ed."

Honest Ed puts a hand on my arm. "Shit, Charlie. I always liked you . . . the guy's a nasty piece of work, you know that."

"And what am I, a bloody Care Bear?"

"I think you want to be wary, that's all."

"I appreciate the advice," I say. "I'll take it on board."

"Make sure you do," Ed says, sipping his pint. "Personally I hope the scumbag burns. Horrible what he did to that woman. I hate to think what'll happen if they find the daughter."

"There was a daughter?" I ask, playing dumb.

"Yeah, had to be a witness," Ed says. "Word is she snuck out while Duffy was doing his thing. Either way, poor girl won't last long once the pigs find her."

I spin a red on the table between finger and thumb. "What makes you say that?"

"Come on Charlie, how many coppers have you paid off to get at a witness? Information and loyalty. The two cheapest commodities on the market."

"Suppose I have been out of it too long," I say, moving on my way. I nod to Posh John and make my way out through the club.

"Mind how you go, Charlie," Ed shouts after me. "You've shown your face, now. People'll be talking."

"I know you will, Ed," I say, walking out of the club.

I return to the car. Ji-min is at the end of the ice cream. I take out a tissue, spit on it and wipe her mouth and fingers.

I get the feeling Ed is telling the truth for once. If Duffy thinks there's a witness, Ji-min isn't safe anywhere. Especially not down the cop shop.

I look at Ji-min and sigh. What the hell am I gonna do with her? Dumping her on Mandy and Cassie is out. It's not safe for them, and besides, they're still on holiday in Marbella.

I screw up the tissue and toss it in a bin in the car park. I slide behind the wheel and give the problem some thought. But not too long. Word will be travelling fast about my return.

9

"Now you see, this one has the ISOFIX, the adjustable headrest . . . and, because safety is paramount . . . side-impact protection, too." The young guy in the purple store t-shirt points out the features of the second, more expensive booster seat. "Plus, should the young lady get thirsty—*ta-da*, cup holder."

I stand in the aisle of the hardware superstore with Ji-min clinging onto my hand, Mr Moo clutched to her chest.

"Mind if I try it out?" I ask.

The store assistant looks up at me. "Uh, I don't think you'll fit— "

"Not me, you numpty," I say.

"Oh yeah, right," the assistant says.

I break Ji-min's grip, grab the show model seat off its shelf and set it down in the middle of the aisle. Picking her up, I place her in the chair. And strap the twin belts over her shoulders.

I clip 'em in place, adjust the headrest and give Ji-min a thumbs-up. "Comfy?"

"Comfy," she says, a thumbs-up in return.

"Uh, is your wife Korean or something?" the assistant asks, giving me a funny look.

"She's adopted," I say.

The assistant seems impressed. "That's very good of you."

"I like to do my bit," I say, sizing up the car seats. "Okay, I think we'll take posh one."

"Excellent choice, sir," the assistant says. "I'll get a boxed one from the back."

"Don't bother," I say, "this one'll do."

"But this is a demo," he says.

"Ex-demo," I correct him, picking up the chair.

I carry Ji-min in the seat as far as the checkout. I hold her up for the girl to scan the barcode on the tag.

Ji-min loves it. Wants to do it again. I carry her out to the car, parked nearby on the retail park.

Fastening Ji-min in, I check the seat is secure.

Ji-min looks sad.

"What's the matter?" I ask. "Not that I'm complaining, but you seem quiet."

Her eyes search mine. "When's Mum coming back?"

Punch me in the face. Kick me in the ribs. Beat me over the head with a cricket bat. Anything but ask me those kinda questions with those kinda eyes.

"Here, watch your cartoons," I say, handing Ji-min her tablet. I plug in her headphones and slip them over her head. Her eyes glue themselves to the screen—something called 'Frozen'.

It seems to ease her pain, so I shut the door and go to walk around the car to the driver's side.

But I spoke too soon about the comparative joys of a beating. I hear the thump of sprinting feet too late. Turn and take a knuckle sandwich on the chin and fall back against the car.

A pair of big lads in dark sportswear and gold chains jump on me, fists flying.

I block the best I can and grab hold of a gold chain around one of the bugger's necks.

I pull him forward and drive my crown into his face. He staggers. His mate swings. I block and counter with a left, right back in the fight.

But Gold Chain hits me again. I spin around. My face driven into the passenger window.

Ji-min sits oblivious on the other side of the glass, singing her lungs out.

She doesn't see or hear me. But I spot one of the guys pull a knife in the light reflecting off the window.

As he lunges with the blade, I turn his mate into the path off the weapon. He takes one in the kidney. By the time his mate frees the blade, I'm already on him, reversing the knife into his guts.

A second head-butt floors him. He hits the tarmac and cradles the butt of the knife.

Meanwhile. Gold Chain hobbles away, a hand to his bleeding wound. Blood spots the floor as he attempts to run towards a white Subaru Impreza with the front doors left open.

I stride after the guy and catch up with him as he reaches the car. I ram his face into the door frame. He almost blacks out. I flip him over against the car and stick a thumb in his wound.

He coughs blood. Cries in agony.

"Who for?"

He shakes his head.

I press harder. *"Who for?"*

"Rudenko," he says, teeth painted red.

I let him go. He flops behind the wheel. The Subaru lurches away, doors still open.

His mate with the knife in his guts speed-hobbles across the car park, intercepts the Subaru and catches a ride. The doors to the Impreza slam shut. It speeds away with a screech of tyres and disappears around the nearest roundabout.

I hurry to the hire car. Shoppers gawping. The police sure to be on their way.

As I round the Peugeot and climb in the driver seat, Ji-min is none the wiser.

She murders some bloody song called *"Let It Go."* Christ, she sounds like a cat being fed into a mincer.

"I'll let you bloody go in a minute," I grumble in the rear view mirror.

She doesn't hear.

I pull out of the car park and get on the main road.

Ivan Rudenko. Word must have got to him. And that pathetic excuse for an ambush will be just the start.

anchester, 1998
We sit across from each other. The girl and me, eating cheese on toast. About as good as my cooking skills get.

My living room has two old armchairs, a TV and an electric fire that stinks when it first comes on. But the girl is in shock and needs warming up.

She wanted to go to the pigs. I told her it wasn't an option. The only option is to sit here and wait.

So that's what we do. The girl wrapped in a blanket, crunching on a piece of toast, trying not to burn her lips on molten cheese slices.

"What's your name?" I ask.

"Yunjin," she says.

"How old are you?"

"Eighteen."

"And where are your family?" I ask.

"I don't have," Yunjin says.

"No mum or dad? Brother or sister?"

Yunjin shakes her head. "No longer."

I bite into a piece of toast and burn my lip. I shake it off, pretending it didn't hurt. "So where are you from, China or somewhere?"

"South Korea," Yunjin says. "After I escape North Korea."

"Escape?"

"You don't know North Korea?"

"Didn't do much school."

"It's not nice place," Yunjin says. "I live on street there, parents dead. South Korea not nice for refugee. So I come here. Try get job. But English not good."

"It's better than most of the dickheads around here," I say.

Yunjin shoots me a nervous glance over her toast, as if she wants to ask me something.

"Go on," I say. "Spit it out."

Yunjin looks at me, confused. She spits her mushed-up toast onto her plate.

"No, it's a saying. It means tell me what you're thinking."

Yunjin rests her plate on her lap. "Why you do this?"

"Do what?"

"Help me."

"I dunno, I just did it."

"Now you in trouble?"

"We both are," I say, taking another bite. "That's why we've got to keep our heads down. Wait for a call."

"Call?"

"From the boss."

"What your boss do?"

I pause as I chew. "Whatever it is, it won't be pretty."

"Then why wait?" Yunjin asks. "Why not run?"

"We run, they find, they kill," I say, as simple as I can. "This way there's a chance. Maybe I can cut a deal."

"You hand me over?" Yunjin asks, worried.

"No," I say. "You stay here. I go and see the boss. But no handing over."

"Why you do this for me?"

"If a girl wants to go on the game, that's her lookout," I say. "But no one's forcing no one to do nothing." I set down my plate and brush the crumbs off my lap. "That's not how it should work."

"You're very brave," Yunjin says, chewing her last piece of toast.

"Yeah, or really fucking stupid."

I pick up my mug and take a sip of my brew.

There's a sudden noise. I almost spill my tea. I look at Yunjin and she looks at me. We turn towards the kitchen.

The phone on the wall continues to ring.

I wait outside the boss' office. He's making me wait on purpose. He always does it, the tosser. Makes the old fart feel important. I suppose he is.

Dwyer is Manchester's biggest crime boss. Expanding his empire across the North West.

He's got designs on the rest of the country too. He has big plans for me, he says.

I could be running my own city, he tells me. If I keep on the way I am. Which makes my antics at the Clubhouse even more daft. But I did it, didn't I? We'll see what his plans are for me now.

I lean against the wall with my hands in the pockets of my black bomber jacket. Flanked by the Two Tony's.

There's Tony G and Tony B. A lofty pair of ex-coppers with moustaches. One is dark-haired, the other ginger. Otherwise, it's hard to tell 'em apart.

They wear cheap suits and stand with their hands folded, like I'm gonna kick 'em in the balls or something. I'll be honest, I've thought about it.

Normally, the Tony's would make small talk. But today, I'm the enemy. So the chit-chat's put on hold. Just the way I like it. I'd rather make enemies than conversation.

Tony and Tony scowl at me like I just shagged their birds. But it's not long before they get the shout. A muffled yell comes from behind a solid wood door.

I straighten up. Tony B, the ginger, opens the door. Tony G nods for me to enter.

I walk through into the boss's gloomy office. It's a big room. High ceilings and way more space than he needs. It's a long walk to his desk, with a window to the left looking out over the factory floor.

Jimmy Dwyer is the head of the Dwyer family. The most notorious crime gang around. He sits behind his big oak desk in his high leather chair. Dressed in pin stripes with a cigar in his mouth, his hair is a balding grey. A pair of bushy sideburns are still alive from the seventies. He looks like a right tosser. But no one'll dare tell him.

I cross the office floors with the Tony's in tow, the air thicker than tar.

Lenny lurks in the corner, fury in his eyes. I ignore the weasel, stop in front of the desk and wait.

Dwyer stubs the end of his cigar in an ashtray. He shakes his head. "I ought to be angry," he says in his deep Irish accent. "No, I am. I am angry. Fucking furious . . ." He looks up at me through a wisp of smoke. "But more disappointed is what I am, Charlie."

I stay quiet.

Dwyer shrugs. "You got nothing to say then?"

I shake my head.

"No 'sorry, Mr Dwyer'," the boss says. "No, 'please forgive me, Mr Dwyer. I didn't mean to kill two of your best fucking men. I didn't mean to chase Lenny out of a fucking window. My nephew. Your fucking captain'."

I shrug. "I'm sorry, Mr Dwyer."

"Yeah? Well sorry's not good enough, son." Dwyer leans back in his chair and shakes his head. "So how are we gonna sort this out, then?"

Lenny steps forward, sneering at me. "I say we sort this soft cunt out— "

"No one asked you," Dwyer snaps at Lenny. "Get back in your fucking corner."

Lenny appeals. *"But— "*

"But nothing," Dwyer says. "And don't think you're out of the doghouse either, 'cause you're not," Dwyer jabs a fat finger at Lenny. "Trying to rape a wee girl, you're a fucking disgrace to this family."

Lenny backs out of the conversation like the lapdog he is.

Meanwhile, Dwyer eyeballs me. "On the one hand, you should be a dead man. On the other, I'd be pretty fucking stupid to dispense with my biggest nuke." Dwyer pushes up out of his chair. He paces to the window and talks to the glass. "We've expanded more since you came on-board than the past twenty years. The very mention of your name gets business done." Dwyer turns from the window and looks at me. "So I'm gonna give you a free pass this time. A one-off ticket out of the shite."

Dwyer ambles back to his desk. I wait for the punchline.

He sinks back into his chair. "Just bring us the girl and we'll forget all about it."

"The girl's not a threat to you," I say.

"The girl's a potential time bomb," Dwyer replies. "And

besides, look at what she did to my wee nephew's face," Dwyer says, pointing to the claw marks on Lenny's face. "As if the ugly stick wasn't enough."

"I'm scarred for life," Lenny says.

"Alright, don't be over-dramatic," Dwyer says, shooting Lenny down. "So, Charlie, are you gonna hand her over or what?"

"I'm sorry for the inconvenience, Mr Dwyer. Maybe I overreacted."

Dwyer huffs. "That's putting it mildly."

"But the girl's off-limits," I say.

"Off-limits? I think your brain is running away with your mouth, sunshine. I say what's off-limits, son. You say will that be all, boss."

I shake my head. "Not this time ... *boss*."

Lenny cracks a smile. He's wanted me out of the picture since day one. "You're dead, you cunt. Dead— "

"For the last time, shut your fucking mouth," Dwyer yells at Lenny. "Or so help me God—" Dwyer calms himself. Turns his attention back to me. "Last chance, Charlie. Or you know what happens next."

I don't move. Don't talk.

"Use your noggin for once rather than your fists," Dwyer says. "No sense in you both wearing a coffin on your back."

I look around the office. At Lenny. The Two Tony's. At Dwyer. "We finished here? I think I left the iron on."

I turn to leave.

"Walk out of here and it's over," Dwyer yells after me. *"You're over!"*

I stride across the office floor. Open the door. Turn and look back at Dwyer.

Ever feel you're making a big mistake, but can't stop yourself?

This is one of those times.

But I go ahead anyway and make the mistake.

I close the door behind me, walk along the corridor and ride the goods lift down to factory level. I hurry across the floor of the meatpacking plant.

Huge vents whir, conveyor belts churn. Factory workers in protective white gear scurry about their business.

The floor is bright red to hide the colour of blood. I look up and see Dwyer watching me from his office.

Of course, they won't try and take me here. They're smarter than that.

No, they'll gather the troops and tool up first. Then they'll come after the both of us. Me and Yunjin.

Together or separate, it doesn't matter. They'll hunt us down. Cut us up like the meat on those conveyors. And make a right royal example.

I've gotta get back to the flat before Dwyer can dispatch a crew, so I break into a sprint as I leave the factory.

I run across the car park to my black Vauxhall Calibra. It's a twenty-minute drive across town. I can do it in fifteen.

That's fifteen minutes to figure out what the hell I'm gonna do.

11

I've no choice but to take Ji-min with me. After all, there's a snitch on every corner, on every hotel desk. The closer to my side, the safer she is.

But she can't see what I'm about to do. So I lie her down in the boot, her head on a pillow and a blanket draped over her.

It helps that she's knackered. Can't keep her bloody eyes open. She drifts right off. I close the boot, as soft as I can. She'll be alright for a while. And I left instructions on what to do if she wakes up and I'm not back.

The ski flap in the backseat is open. The car locked from the outside. But Ji-min can open the doors from the inside. A burner phone is in the compartment under the central arm rest. The phone number of Mandy written on a slip of paper. She works for a man I can trust in Chinatown.

But I'm sure it won't come to that. In fact, I'm aiming to be in and out in five minutes.

I check my watch. It's ten at night and dark as a serial killer's soul. Cold, too. Breath fogging the air and a frost forming over the pavement.

I leave the car in a quiet spot around the corner and enter O'Malley's. It's an Irish dive with live football on the TV and a fruit machine in a corner. There's a long bar with old punters supping Guinness on high stools.

I call the bar lady aside. A large redhead with a stern face and a baggy black Meatloaf t-shirt.

"Bill Duffy been in tonight?"

She shakes her head. "Don't know the name."

"Where can I find him?" I ask, slipping her a tenner.

She pushes it back across the bar top. "I told you, I don't know the name."

Her eyes dart towards a door marked *Private*, to the far end of the bar. I notice there's a camera above the door keeping tabs on events.

"I'll talk to the organ grinder then," I say, taking back my ten pound note and walking towards the door.

I notice it's code-locked. No bother. I step back and kick it in. Two strong boots do the trick,

The door splinters and swings open. The locals carry on drinking, eyes on the football. Nothing new for them and confirmation the place is dodgy. But the redhead looks worried. Like she doesn't know what to do.

I step into a short, narrow corridor with another couple of doors. One leads down to the beer kegs. The other hides a light behind a frosted window.

Terence O'Malley, Manager is etched on the glass, like he's some kind of big deal.

I open the door and find a guy behind a desk. He's halfway through dialling a number, receiver in hand. Any money it isn't the police he's calling.

He puts down the receiver. An average bloke in his forties with what my daughter would call a 'dad bod'.

"What do you want?" he asks, in a thick Irish accent that

reminds me of my old boss, Dwyer. O'Malley looks at me from under a mess of black hair. He has the craggy red face of a drinker.

"You must be Terence," I say.

"That's right."

"You know a man called Bill Duffy?"

O'Malley shakes his head. Swallows deep.

"I'll take that as a yes," I say, pacing around the small, stuffy office, the smell of whiskey from an open bottle on O'Malley's desk. "Where can I find him?"

"Like I said— "

I stop and sigh. "Let's not do the easy way or the hard way thing. I'm tired, and you can't spare the bones."

Terence hesitates in his chair, caught between two evils.

I pick up the bottle of whiskey. Halfway empty. I sniff the top. "Nice," I say. "Shame to waste it."

O'Malley looks confused. I decide he needs some enlightening. So I empty the remaining booze in a nearby office bin.

O'Malley reacts. *"Oi, that cost fifty quid."*

"It's about to cost you more," I say, holding the bottle by the neck.

I smash the base against the desk. Shards fly. O'Malley cowers. He tries to slip out of the office, but I cut him off.

"You know who I am?" I ask, brandishing the bottle.

O'Malley shakes his head.

"You ever hear the name Breaker?"

O'Malley's eyes grow to the size of planets. The gout drains right out of his face. He swallows his own voice.

"Let's get down to brass tacks," I say, pushing O'Malley against the wall. "You know where Bill Duffy is and you're gonna tell me, right now."

"I don't think you get it," O'Malley says, eyeing the jagged base of the bottle. "This is a drop bar."

Shit, that's not good.

"And Bill Duffy is protected," O'Malley continues. "From upon fucking high." He senses the hesitation in me. "If you are who you say you are, you'll know what that means."

"And if this is a drop bar, you can tell me who makes the pickups."

"One of Murphy's crews," O'Malley says.

Bollocks.

"The same guys protecting Bill Duffy," O'Malley says.

Shit, shite, bugger and bollocks.

I pause with the bottle in hand, weighing up what I'm about to do. This changes everything. And yet changes nothing.

I grab O'Malley by the collar and slam the side of his head down against the desk. I raise the bottle. "You've got one chance . . . One question. One answer."

"I'm fucked either way," O'Malley says, breathing fast and shallow.

"You can be fucked right now, or fucked later, it's up to you."

O'Malley hesitates.

"Alright then," I say swinging the bottle.

"Wait!" the guy yells, waving a hand in surrender. I stop the broken bottle millimetres from his jugular.

He trembles in my grip. "He's at the bowling alley."

"Which one?"

"Mega Bowl."

"You sure he's there now?"

"As sure as I can be," O'Malley says.

"How do you know?"

"Cause he loves fucking bowling. What do you think?"

O'Malley winces under my grip. "It's a Murphy front. He's running the place. Running it into the ground if you ask me, but that's where you'll find the arsehole."

I let O'Malley go. He gasps for air and flops into his desk chair. I ditch the broken bottle in the whiskey-filled bin.

As I close the office door behind me, the barmaid appears in the corridor.

"Sorry about the door," I say on my way out.

12

Manchester, 1998

I live in one of the inner city high rises. One of a block of six towers. A right fucking jungle. The perfect place to live under the radar of the law. And a stone's throw from where I do most of my work.

Trouble is, it's seventeen stories up. And the lift's out again. Someone kicked the pissing door in. Probably a speed-freak or meth head.

If I catch 'em doing it, I'm gonna drop 'em off the roof. In the meantime, I've gotta run up flight after flight. Until I hit the fifteenth.

My feet pound over the concrete flags as I run along the open-air corridor down the side of the building.

I open the door and race inside. Find Yunjin curled up on my bed, sleeping. She startles awake as I fling open the door on the old, cheap, freestanding wardrobe.

Yunjin rubs her eyes. "What's wrong?"

"A lot's fucking wrong." I grab my emergency bag from the bottom of the wardrobe. It's pre-packed. Clothes, cash and a handgun.

Passport too. 'Cause you never know.

I swing the bag over a shoulder. "You live near here?"

"Uh, I think so."

"Yes or no?"

"I live Moss Side."

"That's a no, then," I reply. "But it's close enough. Come on."

I drag Yunjin off the bed.

She resists. "You still not say what's wrong."

"It's what I thought. They want me to hand you over," I say.

"Who wants?"

"My boss . . . Jimmy Dwyer."

"Who are they?"

"Oh, no one," I say, pulling her through the flat to the front door. "Only the head of the biggest mafia outfit in Manchester."

I drag Yunjin through the flat, out through the front door.

She pulls away. "Please no. No hand over."

I yank her in close with one hand, locking the door to the flat with the other. "I told you, that's not gonna happen."

She looks in my eyes. Sees I'm legit. I check over the balcony. Scan the front courtyard and the car park for signs of trouble. I don't see any. So we run.

But wait.

The tower overlooks a flyover. Part of the ring-road, noisy with the rush of traffic.

I spot a pair of black Jags peeling off and pulling into the tower car park at speed. They brake to a stop alongside each other. Tooled-up heavies jump out with that look in their eye. And that fucking weasel, Lenny, leading the hunting party.

They run towards the front entrance. It's not locked. Never locked.

The situation doesn't take any explaining. Yunjin tenses up, gripping my hand tight as we watch the men enter the tower.

I pull her onwards. We make it to the stairs and I push her up another flight.

"What are we doing? The way out is down."

"Yeah, and the way in is up," I say, shoving her through the door for the sixteenth floor.

I hold the door handle closed and peer through the thin, tall slit of wired glass.

Dwyer's boys know I'm on the fifteenth. I can hear them running, climbing, barking instructions.

I back Yunjin up into a corner next to the doorway. "Get down," I tell her. She crouches low in the shadows as I return to the window in the door.

They'll head for the fifteenth. But if I was them, I'd leave at least one guy in the stairwell and send a couple of scouts to flush out the levels above and below.

I hear 'em getting close. And that's exactly what Lenny is yelling at 'em to do.

So I edge away from the door. Stand on the inside of it. In seconds, a man bundles through. His name is Chris Courtenay. A black ex-cruiser-weight with a right-hook like a sledgehammer.

I take him by surprise, ramming his head into the wall.

He reacts. A winding thump in my guts. A couple of 'em. I drive an elbow in his back. Scoop him up and spear-tackle him face-first into the concrete.

There's a crack as his neck breaks. I drop Courtenay's body and drag a horrified Yunjin through the door.

I leave her on the landing with my bag while I sprint down the next flight of stairs.

There's a second guy stationed as lookout outside the door to the fifteenth. He's packing a shooter, but slow to react. I kick the gun from his hand and boot him in the chest. He tumbles down the stairs and comes to a stop on the seat of his pants. I'm not far behind. And as he picks himself up, I drive a knee into his jaw.

It sparks him out. I bound back up the stairs and wave Yunjin down. She struggles with the weight of the holdall. I take the bag off her and we hurry down the fourteenth.

We come across a scout coming out through one of the stairwell doors. I shoulder it hard, trapping him between door and wall.

He cries out and reaches for his pistol. I knock him dizzy with a right to the chin.

He drops. We run. All the way down to the bottom.

I hear more yelling above as Lenny and the boys find their injured pals.

We push through the ground floor. Yunjin goes to run across the courtyard. I drag her back and steer her round the side of the building.

At the back of the block is a long strip of wild bushes and grass. What passes for nature round here, littered with all the crap you can imagine. We pick our way through the the bottles, shopping trolleys, bottomed-out sofas and rusting fridges.

We come out into a narrow road between the bushes and a graffitied wall topped with barbed wire. My Calibra is parked out of sight on the road. I throw the bag in the boot and we jump inside. I fire the car up and reverse fast.

I pull the handbrake and spin the wheel as the road

widens out. The car flips round ninety degrees. I slip it into
first and spin the tyres.

They bite and we pull clear of the tower, Yunjin pinned
back in her seat, gripping tight to the door handle.

I hare down a network of side roads. Little cut-throughs
I know between council estate roads. It brings us back out
under the flyover. I take the ramp onto the ring-road and
merge in with the traffic.

"What's your address?" I ask Yunjin.

They've already scoped it out. Fuck knows how they
found out.

"You fill in a form when you applied for that
job?" I ask, sitting low behind the wheel.

"Form?"

"You tell 'em your name, where you live, all that shit?"

"Uh, yes," Yunjin says.

That explains it.

I check again in the rear view mirror, making sure no
one blind-sides us. We're parked around on the corner of
Yunjin's street—a Victorian house share with a bunch of
other refugees. A real slum-hole in the middle of an estate
crawling with dealers and pimps.

On the corner, I can see everyone who comes and goes.
And get a good view of the car outside her house, without
them seeing us in return.

Dwyer has a B-team sitting outside in a grey BMW. Two
guys wander out of the front door they only just kicked in.
They shake their heads and climb back in the car.

I'm hoping they'll drive off. But they sit and wait.

"Getting your stuff is out of the question," I say.

"I need things," Yunjin says. "I have little money. Clothes. Photos. Passport."

"Forget 'em," I say.

Yunjin flaps her arms. "But I have nothing."

"You have your health," I say. "You want less? Be my guest."

"Be my what—?"

"Point is," I say. "This means we're both fucked."

"Why?" Yunjin asks.

"'Cause you can't go anywhere without your passport. And I'm not going anywhere without you."

"We can hide," Yunjin says. "Stay in UK."

"Nah," I say, shaking my head. "It was a stupid idea anyway. They would have caught up with us sooner or later . . . Running never works."

"How can you know?"

"'Cause I'm the guy they send after you when you do."

"You can't chase self," Yunjin says.

"No, but they can send some real heavy hitters after us. Or if they've got any brains, get the coppers to do it for 'em."

"You bribe police here, too?" Yunjin asks.

"Don't have to," I say. "They've got a menu of services and prices. Anything for a slice of the pie."

"Then what we do now?" Yunjin asks. "You want me gone? This not your fault."

"It's no one's fault but that shit-stain, Lenny."

"Little man with small dick?" Yunjin asks.

I burst out laughing. "Yeah, that's him . . . You know you left a right fucking mark on the dickhead."

"Huh?"

"Scratches," I say, pretending to claw at my face.

"I not sorry," Yunjin says.

"You shouldn't be, either," I say, watching the street. "It's a big improvement."

"So what we do?" Yunjin asks. "Can't sit here forever."

"No, we can't," I say with a sigh.

I chew on it a minute. Then I get an idea. I tell Yunjin to stay put.

"You know how to drive?" I ask.

"I had a few lessons, back in Korea."

"Then take the wheel," I say. "Come and pick me up."

Yunjin seems unsure. "Pick up? When?"

"You'll know when," I say, taking my handgun from under my jacket.

I open the driver-side door and climb out. Hold my gun low and close to my side. Jog round the corner and along the street.

Dwyer's goons are too busy watching the house. They don't see me coming until it's too late.

I run up behind the BMW. A door opens. I take out the driver with a headshot. The bullet passes through his skull and shatters the window.

The front passenger jumps out, but I'm already firing. He takes one in the shoulder and stumbles back. I fire twice in his chest. He falls back over a low-lying wall, into the front yard of the house.

That leaves goon number three. He's on the backseat. He slips low out of a rear door.

I drop lower and see him crouching on the other side of the car. I whistle. He turns.

I shoot under the belly of the car and get the fucker in the kneecap. He yelps like a dog. I rise and slide over the bonnet of the BMW.

The guy's on one leg, his back turned, weapon in hand. I whistle again. He spins and takes aim. But not before I land a bullet in his right shoulder. He drops his weapon. Hangs on to the car door. I move in fast and flip him around against the car. I point the gun in his face. He whimpers from the pain.

"Tell Dwyer I want to make this right. I'll meet him between the old mills. Six o'clock tonight. Got it?"

The guy nods.

"Good," I say, punching him hard in the ribs.

He collapses to the kerb.

As I step out onto the road, I tuck the gun away. I wave an arm high over my head. The Calibra lurches around the corner. It jerks and swerves, gears crunching. But it makes it down the street, passenger door open. I cross the street and wait. As the Calibra rolls by, I jump in and swing the door shut. I drum on the dash, *"Go, go, go!"*

Yunjin steps on the accelerator. We make it down the street in the wrong gear and around the next bend. She almost totals the car twice, but we're clear.

Doubt anyone in the neighbourhood'll blab about the shooting. They'll know those are Dwyer's boys. And the filth'll cover it up anyway.

I swap seats with Yunjin and take control of the car. I put my foot down and we speed away.

13

I check on Ji-min. She's awake. Wants out of the boot. Won't take go back to sleep for an answer.

I lift her out and set her down on the car park.

"Plus I need a wee," she says, dancing on the spot.

"Come on then," I say leading her across the car park to the bright lights of the Mega Bowl.

She grabs my hand as we walk. I'm trying not to encourage it. Don't want her to get too attached. But I let her have my hand this once.

I pull the door open. Make a beeline straight for the toilets.

It's half-busy. The usual layout. A foyer, desk and a games arcade to the left, alongside a bar and a set of table and chairs where people can order fast food.

Then a dozen lanes at the far end. An ear-bashing blend of pop music, arcade machines and the hollow clatter of downed skittles.

I've been here a few times, so I know where the toilets are. "You okay on your own?" I ask Ji-min outside the door to the ladies.

"I'm five," she says, as if that's any kind of answer.

I help her push the door open and head off for a wazz myself. When I emerge, Ji-min is coat-tailing a woman out of the door.

"You hungry?" I ask.

She shakes her head.

"Good, then let's get you back in the— "

Ji-min locks on to something across the carpet. A kid's ride. A rocking pink unicorn playing some godawful song.

She runs over and climbs on the ride.

Oh, for Christ's sake.

I dig my hand in a pocket and follow her over. *"Two quid?"*

"Pleeeaase, Uncle Charlie."

"Bloody criminal," I say, jamming a couple of coins in the slot.

The ride starts. Ji-min is lost in some imaginary unicorn-pony trance. Reminds me of Cassie, when she was a similar age. We came here a few times. Cassie, her mum and me. I'd have to gutter every ball on purpose to make sure she won, otherwise there'd be tears and ice cream required. Cassie would get upset, too, ha-ha . . . I guess you had to be there.

But anyway, with Ji-min occupied by the ride, I scan the alley for signs of Wild Bill. He's not out on the floor. So either O'Malley was lying, or the guy's hiding away in the back.

As Ji-min's ride comes to an end. I notice a couple of kids jumping in and out of a ball pool. There's a soft-play area too. All self-contained within nets and tucked away among the arcade machines.

"Fancy a go in there?" I ask her, pointing at the ball pool.

She nods. I lift her down off the ride and escort her over.

"Here, let's take off your shoes," I say bending down. I

undo the Velcro straps on her silver trainers and pull them off one by one. "Stay here 'til I get back, okay?"

"Where are you going?" Ji-min asks.

"To say hello to someone . . . Don't wander off, okay?"

"Okay," Ji-min says, stepping through the nets. She launches herself into the ball pool, turns, turns and waves.

I wave back, tuck her shoes under a bench and stride off across the bowling alley carpet.

I pace up and down the alleys, checking each lane for signs of Wild Bill.

When I don't see him, I head for the reception desk. There's a teenage beanpole in glasses spraying shoes.

"Alright," I say.

He grunts and sprays.

"Bill Duffy working tonight?"

"No, why?"

"I'm an old mate, that's all. When will he be back in?"

"He's in tonight," the lad says, slipping the shoes back inside their slot.

"Thought you said he wasn't here."

The lad sighs, a mouth full of metal. "You asked if he was working tonight. Not if he was here."

I stare at the lad. He stares at me. "Lane twelve," he says, spraying another set of shoes.

"I just came from there," I say. "No sign of him."

The lad shrugs and sighs some more. "What do you want from me? I spend my nights spraying poisonous chemicals on people's foot cheese." He sprays again, but the can comes up empty. The lad slumps in the shoulders. "Great, now I've gotta go and get some more."

As the lad trudges off in search of another can, I stand in the middle of the Mega Bowl, chewing over my options.

And that's when I see him. Wild Bill Duffy. It's been a few years, but he's still got the same spud-shaped head. The same horrible scowl. He wears jeans and a white polo shirt. Walks like a hyena in the grass. Hunched in the shoulders, carrying a tray of fast food and sucking on a drink through a straw.

Hiding behind a pillar as he crosses my path, I spin out behind him and pick up his tail. Back towards the alley at the end of the line.

Murphy will have told him to stay out of public. And I know Duffy will have got sloppy, lazy, cocky . . . Like they all do.

Well one man's arrogance is another man's opportunity. I catch him up. Only ten yards behind, feeling a rising tide inside.

Rage, I guess you'd call it.

My hands squeeze into fists, eyes locked on the back of his shaved, lumpy skull. He reaches the end of the line and sets his tray down on the standing table at the back of the lane.

Duffy picks up the hot dog, brings it to his mouth and takes a bite. He freezes as he spots me. He knows who I am. And he'll have already gotten word.

The rest seems to happen in slow motion. The hot dog falling from Duffy's hands as I approach. His body turning to run. Me standing big. Standing ready. Ready to grab him when he passes by.

Except he breaks sideways, out onto the lane. He hops onto the next one, dodging a rolling ball.

I run to intercept. But he's in bowling shoes and I'm in boots. I slip and land on my back. Duffy hurdles over me. I scramble to my feet, slipping and sliding.

Duffy hops from one lane to the other as I run with all the speed I have. But the slick, polished lanes betray me.

Bowling balls, too. I jump over a speeding green ball and go arse over tit as I land, flopping like a walrus on a slab of ice.

Duffy tries to get off the lanes. Slips over too. But he's up fast. I grab an orange ball off a woman as I make it off the lane. I hurl it at the bastard. But I miss. It smashes into a sweet machine, sending tiny little rainbow balls all over the floor.

Duffy disappears between arcade machines. I'm close behind. But I lose sight of him in the walls of games flashing and wailing and spitting out jackpots of change.

I move around the machines. He's hiding in here some-where. *I know it.*

I round the side of a block of fruit machines. See him hiding behind an F1 racing game. He's eyeing the exit. Thinking of making a run for it.

He doesn't hear me coming for him.

All I need to do is grab him, knock him out and get him out of here and in the boot. I can run back in for Ji-min before someone calls any kind of police or security.

So I sneak up behind. Getting closer. And closer. *But shit.* Men entering the bowling alley. Three of 'em dressed in black. I know a hit squad when I see one. And I know those men.

They belong to Ivan Rudenko. Murphy's old rival. The man I helped put away. The man who used to run half this city.

O'Malley made the call. Put the word out. And here they come. Armed and ready to shoot me down.

One of Rudenko's boys spots me creeping up behind

Duffy. He points and yells to his two mates. Duffy turns and sees me.

The little shit's one of life's chancers. He knows a window of opportunity when he sees one. And he jumps right through it, scurrying past Rudenko's men and out of the entrance.

Meanwhile, the hit squad is heading my way with weapons drawn by their sides. They're here to kill me and they don't mind who knows it.

I step round the back of the racing game and see the lad from the desk carrying a new can of foot spray. I snatch it off him. He doesn't have the energy to argue. I shove him aside. "Get out of here."

I pull my lighter from my jacket and flip it open. But on second thoughts, no. The arcade area is full of people. Too dangerous.

I tuck my lighter away and hide alongside the bank of fruit machines. I peer round the corner and see Rudenko's men fan out.

The first one comes my way. I wait with the can.

As he appears round the corner, I spray him in the eyes, his cries lost in the din of the arcade. The guy drops his gun and collapses blind to his knees.

I look for the pistol. It's under one of the machines. My hand too big for the gap. So I punch the guy hard in back of his neck. He goes to sleep. I move on at the sight of the next hitman.

The arcade is a whirl of lights and sounds, enough to make you dizzy. I duck low next to a shoot-em-up game, one of a pair.

As the next guy approaches, I retreat into the gap between shoot-em-ups. The bloke is a middle-aged lug with a bald head. He looks from one machine to the other, senses on high alert.

I wait until he's in front of me with his back turned. Then I emerge, draw a big blue arcade gun from its slot and hold it to the back of his skull.

"Drop it," I say.

He drops his shooter.

The arcade game gun is fixed to a long metal chord. I wrap it around the guy's throat and pull him back into the gap between machines.

I throttle him to sleep, his feet kicking until they don't anymore.

Leaving him in the shadows, I step back out onto the floor. I snatch the guy's gun from the carpet before anyone spots it. And I go hunting. The remaining assassin my prey.

I catch a glimpse of him at the end of the aisle and follow behind. But again, my conscience gets the upper hand.

Real-life shoot-outs mean real-life victims. And I've not got a clear shot. So I raise the gun in the air where people can see me. I fire off three rounds.

Enough to cause panic. A stampede. A distraction. The remaining hitman swept up in the chaos.

I tuck the gun in my jeans and beat a path to the play area, reach inside and scoop Ji-min out of the ball pool. I grab her trainers and run with her tucked under one arm.

We're soon lost in the crowd, screaming and pushing their way through the front entrance.

Then across the car park. To the Peugeot. I put Ji-min in the booster seat and get busy strapping her in.

She's telling me all about the ball pool and the play area. Who did what and how a boy threw a ball at her head and called her fat.

"You're not fat, you're just well-fed,' I say. "Like me."

"Plus he called me ugly," Ji-min adds.

"You're not ugly either," I say, fiddling with the seatbelt, the strap twisted and stuck. "He's just making up for his own insecurities."

"What are insecurities?"

"When other people feel ugly, they look for someone who's pretty to call ugly so they don't feel so ugly anymore. Got it?"

Ji-min nods. "People are mean to other people 'cause they're mean to themselves."

"Exactly," I say. "You know you're pretty smart."

I clip in the belt and glancing over my shoulder. Across the car park, I spot a shadowy figure running my way. He has a weapon in both hands, ready to take a shot.

Bollocks.

The remaining hitman closes the gap to get a better shot. I slip Ji-min's headphones on her head and press play on the tablet. Throwing the door shut, I draw my handgun on the turn.

As Rudenko's man aims, I fire.

He drops to the deck with two bullets in his chest—cue more frantic screams from fleeing customers.

I hurry round the car and jump behind the wheel. The gun stashed in the glovebox and the gearstick in reverse.

Ji-min takes her headphones off. "What are all those bangs?"

"Just balloons popping," I say. "It must be someone's birthday."

"Why is everyone running?" Ji-min asks.

"They're just excited to get home," I say, reversing the car fast out of its space.

The Peugeot bunny hops over the dead hitman's body. "Oops, who left that hippo in the road?" I say.

Ji-min giggles. *"Again!"*

I put the car in first and accelerate. The second bump is even more fun.

14

———

I finally get around to picking up the keys for the serviced apartment I booked while waiting for my flight from JFK.

It's a respectable chain in the city centre round the back of Piccadilly train station.

No reception desk means no one talks or asks questions. I enter a code on a mailbox in the reception area and a door springs open.

There's an envelope inside with a key and a welcome note. We take the lift to the top floor and enter the apartment. It's modern and compact. A studio with caramel furniture, a small strip kitchen and a flatscreen on the wall.

There's a double and a sofa bed, a Wi-Fi connection and a view over Manchester through floor-to-ceiling windows.

I dump my bag on the carpet and remove the gun from my jeans. Tucking it away in a safe built into a sliding wardrobe, I set the code so Ji-min can't see.

As the lock on the safe door whirs, I stretch out tall. Ji-min climbs on the bed and jumps up and down. I shouldn't have let her sleep in the boot of the car. Now she'll be awake half the night. That makes two of us.

I move to the windows and slide one of them open. The cool night air whispers in. I step out onto a thin balcony with a wall that rises to waist-height. The familiar sound of police sirens wail away in the distance. Orange streetlights shimmer on the oily-black surface of the canal. And traffic chugs and honks in a busy stream below.

The city is like an animal. Wild and alive. And if you're not careful, it'll bite your bloody knackers off. But it's, I dunno, captivating.

I hear the pad of feet behind me. Ji-min joins me on the balcony.

She stands and strains on her tiptoes. "I can't see."

I scoop her up in an arm.

She looks across the city in wonder. "Wow, we're so high up."

We take in the view together.

"Why are we so high up?" she asks.

"Because we're on the top floor."

"Why is this the top floor?"

"Because they didn't build any more."

I look at Ji-min, hoping that's the end of it.

Seems like it is. I breathe in the air and soak up the view. A minute's peace, at last.

"Why didn't they build any more?" Ji-min asks.

Oh Christ, I forgot about the dreaded *Why's*.

Cassie was a bugger for it at Ji-min's age.

Why is the sun yellow?

Why do cats have tails?

Why do boys have willies?

My God, it was endless.

"Because they ran out of bricks," I finally say, to quell Ji-min's curiosity.

She screws up her mouth and thinks long and hard over my reply. 'Why didn't they buy enough bricks?"

Shit, I walked right into that one.

"I'm hungry," I say. "Who else here is hungry?"

Ji-min's hand shoots up.

"Come on then," I say, setting her down. "I think I saw some takeaway menus in the kitchen."

We sit eating a Chinese at the table.

I thought it would make Ji-min feel closer to home. And I know. technically she was born in Britain. And Chinese isn't the same as Korean. But they do use chopsticks. Besides, there were only three menus and the place delivers free within a mile.

I wrestle with the sticks for a while until ditching them in favour of a fork.

It's one thing to have Ji-min giggling at me. It's another for the chicken fried rice to slip from the sticks every time I stoop in for a mouthful.

Meanwhile, Ji-min works her sticks like a pro, shuttling sticky rice and dumplings into her mouth with consummate ease.

While we eat, I think about what to do. I'm not about to give up on Duffy. But there's the issue of his connection to Murphy's outfit.

And I know Rudenko. Every failed attempt on my life is only gonna make him more determined to see me dead in the gutter.

And then there's Ji-min. What the hell do I do with her?

I chew and listen to her singing to herself in Korean, her chopsticks ditched, reaching for the tablet.

"Twenty minutes and that's your limit," I say. "You'll go cross-eyed."

"Eyes can't be cross," Ji-min says, looking at the screen.

"Yes they can, look." I turn my pupils inward and pull a funny face.

Ji-min laughs so hard she almost falls off her chair.

I give her half an hour on the tablet and dump the take-away trays in the bin. Plump a pillow, I pull the duvet away from the sheets.

She comes out of the bathroom in white Pokémon pyja-mas, clutching her teddy close to her chest. She hops up into bed and yawns. I tuck her in and she settles down with her head resting on the pillow.

I go to turn off the lamp.

"Uncle Charlie?" Ji-min asks.

"Yeah?"

"Mum's not coming back from heaven, is she?"

"What makes you say that?"

"She would have been back by now. Mum never left me on my own for long."

Bloody hell. This is the conversation I hoped would never come. At least not until I'd palmed her off on someone who knows what to say.

I sit down on the edge of the bed, mind scrambling for the right words. "Your Mum isn't gone," I say. "She goes everywhere you go. And she's here, right now."

"What do you mean?" Ji-min asks, big eyes staring into mine.

"Angels don't have wings or fly around like in drawings or on TV," I say. "They're in here." I point to her chest. "And in here." I tap her on the forehead. "They watch over us from inside, see?"

Ji-min nods.

"So whenever you want your mum, all you need to do is close your eyes and she'll be there."

"What if I can't see her?" Ji-min asks.

"Then you'll feel her in your heart, or in your guts," I say, tapping her on the belly. "Everything you do in life; she'll be there to guide you."

A tear breaks from Ji-min's eye. She wipes it away with a pyjama sleeve.

"Does your angel guide you too, Uncle Charlie?"

"Not all of us get to have angels."

"Why not?"

"Because some of us have done bad things. And I don't think you get an angel if you do bad things."

"But I think now you do good things," Ji-min says.

"Well, I still do bad things, but for better reasons."

"So that means you don't have an angel to look after you?"

"Probably not."

"Don't worry," Ji-min says, putting a hand on my arm. "I will protect you."

I smile at Ji-min. She smiles back.

"I feel safer already," I say, reaching for the lamp. "Now, get to sleep."

"Bedtime story," Ji-min says.

"I don't know any."

"Read something," Ji-min says.

"Like what?"

"Like anything."

Ji-min holds my stare. I'm the first to break.

"Alright, um . . ." I take out my phone and scroll through to the news. "You said *anything*, right?"

Ji-min nods and smiles. Wriggles to get comfortable.

"Okay then." I tap on a story on the Manchester Evening News. As Ji-min clutches Mr Moo to her chin, I start to read. "It was an even match on a crisp autumn evening. United scored twice through Pogba and Lukaku, only for City to come back in the second half with two goals from top scorer, Sergio Aguero. Like all derby encounters, the game started at a furious pace, culminating in a rash of early bookings—
"

I stop and notice Ji-min is in the land of nod, her mouth catching flies.

I read the rest of the article to myself and get up off the bed. I turn off the lamp, casting the room in semi-darkness. The sofa bed is big and long. I don't even bother making it up. Just collapse on my back and kick off my boots. In seconds, I'm gone too.

I check my watch. Ought to be any time now. And the black Honda Accord I noticed last night is still parked up on the street.

Didn't take him long to find me. When it comes to the good private snoops, it never does.

This one's name is Pete. A former detective. His fees pay for his booze. But being half-cut doesn't seem to slow him down.

I wait inside the door to the building and check my watch again. Gotta be any time now, so I open the door and step out onto the pavement. I stride left along the street and pick my way through the busy crossing as people hurry to the train station.

It's a short walk up a wide, rising pedestrian path as far as Piccadilly. I turn right and walk as far as the small Sainsbury's inside. I grab a basket and pick up a couple of pints of milk, a box of Cheerios, a loaf, a block of butter and juice. I throw in a few bananas, chocolate bars, crisps and some cheese slices.

I pay for the food and exit the station.

Coming out the back way, I cut across the car park and out onto the street where the apartments are located.

It's another few minutes' walk in the morning sunshine, but with the front entrance in sight, I notice the Honda is gone.

The rush of tyres over road announce the arrival of a second car. It pulls up fast a few metres in front of me. The car is a long black Mercedes. The biggest money can buy. The front passenger door opens.

A man climbs out, built like a retired rugby player who's had one too many naan breads. He's dressed in a dark suit and sunglasses.

I stop in my tracks. He opens the rear passenger door and waves me into the back.

I check my watch. Seeing as Pete would have fed back my whereabouts late last night, I'd say they're right on cue.

I walk forward and duck my head inside the car.

Connaugh Murphy sits on the far side of the backseat, behind the driver, Lisa. She's a one-time crush of mine. Okay, so a permanent crush.

The man on the pavement is called Trev. We were each other's Secret Santa a couple of years back, when I still went to the Christmas parties of my clients.

"I see you got out of prison then," I say. "You still got the socks?"

"Yeah," he says. "You still using the bottle opener?"

"I've got it somewhere," I say.

"Get in the fucking car," Trev says.

So I get in the fucking car.

Trev slams the door behind me. He's in fast. The Mercedes pulling away from the kerb.

Lisa directs her baby blues my way in the rear view. She looks immaculate as always. Black hair pinned tidy. Cream business suit without a crease. Like the shit slides right off her.

Murphy is just as well turned out. A nuclear tan, a navy suit and a pink open-necked shirt. His customary Fedora hat sits perched on his knee. His silver hair styled in a sweeping quiff, like the young lads have it nowadays. "Charlie," he says in his pretend-posh voice. "How long's it been?"

"Not long enough."

"Funny seeing you here," he continues. "How long have you been back in town?"

"Just flew in," I say.

"Business or pleasure?"

"Visiting relatives," I say.

"Staying long?" Lisa asks.

"Depends," I say. "Got space for dinner if you fancy it."

"Some other time," Lisa says, turning the Mercedes into the next street.

"So Charlie," Murphy says. "What can I do to make your stay more comfortable?"

"Well you can give me a lift to my front door if you want."

Murphy smiles. But I can tell I'm getting on his nerves. You can push it a little with him. But not too far.

He stares out of the window. "A little birdie tells me you went bowling last night."

"Family outing," I say.

"Didn't know you had another daughter," Murphy says.

"Didn't know you had the Korean genes," Lisa adds.

"She's adopted," I say.

"That's nice of you," Murphy says.

"I'm a charitable guy."

"Clearly," Murphy replies. "But even charity has its limits."

"I don't know what you mean, Mr Murphy."

The old man turns to face me. "I'll always be grateful for you putting that fat Russian fuck away."

"Business good is it?"

"Good?" Murphy says. "It's fucking booming. We've doubled in size. Tripled in profits. Diversified our revenue streams. We're just getting started. And it's all thanks to you, Charlie."

"What a heart-warming tale," I say.

Murphy leans in. "Now I want to help you, Charlie."

I roll my eyes. "Here we go."

"Look around," Murphy says, gesturing to the shiny new glass buildings springing up like daffodils. "The city's a lot bigger than it used to be. The Chinese are pouring money in. And we're not confined to Manchester anymore. It's one hell of an opportunity for a man with your expertise."

"Haven't we been down this road before?" I ask. "I seem to remember it hitting a dead end."

"I told you," Lisa says to Murphy, in her soft Irish accent.

He waves a hand in acknowledgement. "Well if I can't tempt you, allow me to enlighten you," Murphy continues, finally getting to the meat in the sandwich. "Bill Duffy is on my payroll."

"Yeah, I heard as much."

"Then it goes without saying that he's not to be touched."

"He wants his balls lopping off."

"I couldn't agree more," Murphy says.

"Then what's the problem?" I ask. "He a blood relative or something?"

"Wife's sister's cousin or some bollocks like that," Murphy says. "But it's not cause the cunt-stain is family, or even that he serves any worthwhile purpose." Murphy toys with the rim of his hat. "He's part of my outfit, Charlie. He's *known*. And if I let some fucker come and take him down, that's not good for the Murphy brand. Unless and until I do something about it. And that involves doing something I don't want to do."

"Something that involves me, I take it."

Murphy turns in his seat to face me. "I'm not protecting Bill Duffy, Charlie. I'm protecting you . . . From yourself."

"I appreciate the concern, Mr Murphy. But there's a real easy way for this to happen."

"Such as?" Murphy asks.

"You hand over Duffy. I do what I have to do. Make it look like a disciplinary handed down from your good self. No one has to know."

Murphy cracks a wistful smile. "I run a tight ship. But it's a big ship these days, Charlie. Leaks happen. And word *always* gets out."

"There's got to be a line," I say.

"You're right," Murphy says, drawing one between us across the seat. "And it's right here."

Lisa makes one left turn after another. We're heading round in one big circle, back towards the spot where they picked me up.

The car rolls to a stop by the kerb. Trev gets out. He opens the rear passenger door.

"Just so we're clear," Murphy says as I'm getting out. "Keep the girl quiet, leave Duffy alone and no harm will come to either of you."

I slide off the backseat with my shopping and get to my feet on the kerb. Trev goes to close the door. I put a hand on the frame and duck my head inside.

"Just so we're clear, you come anywhere near the girl, you'll watch your empire burn. Right before I put that hundred-quid haircut of yours on a fucking spike."

Murphy laughs. "A little dramatic, don't you think?" His eyes darken. "Walk away, Charlie. I mean it."

I take my hand from the door. Trev slams it shut. He gets back in the car. As I walk towards the apartments, the Mercedes pulls past at speed and disappears around the next corner.

I stand outside the apartments and watch it go. Murphy's parting words swim around in my head. The sensible thing to do would be to leave it. To walk away, like the man said.

But sensible doesn't cage the animal. It's angry and it wants out. I reach for the fob to the apartment entrance.

I look up around me, at the skyline, dotted with half-finished glass towers. I ask myself, what would Breaker do?

15

M anchester, 1998

"Go inside," I say, handing Yunjin a small wad of notes. "Order lots of food." I hand her a key. "If I'm not back by dessert, head back to my flat. Pull the washing machine away from the wall. There's a bin bag taped to the back of it with enough cash for you to start a new life."

"But, I can't take your money—" Yunjin says.

"If I'm not back in a couple of hours, the cash'll be no good to me anyway."

"Whatever you're—you don't have to— "

I lean across her and push the passenger door open.

Yunjin hesitates. She can see I'm not for budging. "Thank you," she says, getting out.

I pull the door closed and leave her standing on the pavement outside the restaurant. It's a Chinese place called The Happy Dragon. The food's good and the owner's clean. Besides, it's in China Town, which falls under the rule of the East Asian mafia.

I drive the short distance out of town to a lockup. It's

raining again. A spit turns into a downpour.

The lockup is halfway along a row of blue garage doors, down a cobbled alley full of piss-stains and weeds. I park outside. Run to the door. Unlock it and push it up to the roof.

It's dark inside. Smells of oil and cement. There's a spare car in the middle of the garage under a green tarpaulin. A freestanding steel storage cabinet against a wall. It has two doors. I unlock them both.

Inside is a homemade gun rack and a shelf full of cartridges and magazines in boxes. There's a black holdall at the base of the cabinet. I open it up and pick out a few guns. I find the matching cartridges and magazines—stick 'em in the bag.

I have a big, fuck-off knife attached to the inside of the door. And a baseball bat propped up against the cabinet.

Taking them both for luck, I whip the tarpaulin off the car and snatch the key off a hook on the wall. The bag goes in the boot. The car gets reversed into the lashing rain. The Calibra takes its place and I lock up the storage cabinet and garage door.

I turn on the wipers, turn up the blowers and drive to the end of the alleyway, tyres rumbling over the cobbles. Hopping onto the ring road, I continue the short drive to the meat-packing factory.

It's down a private lane with fields behind hedges either side. I stop halfway down. Reverse and back the car into a gap in a hedge row and check my watch.

You might be thinking why the switch of cars? Why not the Calibra.

Well they'll recognise the Calibra, won't they? And besides, sometimes you need a fast getaway car. Other times you need an ocean-blue Volvo 940.

I check the time on the dash. Almost five. Knocking-off time. The factory staff already finished and done at four.

The thing about Dwyer. He's old. And old grey bastards are predictable. They like their routines. Their tea at eleven. Their cake at three. Their chops on the table and feet in their slippers by the six o'clock news.

I open the zip on the holdall and take out my favourite gun. A sawed-off double-barrel. It's not exactly subtle, but there's just something about it. Maybe it reminds me of myself.

I load the gun and rest it on my lap and slap a clip in the Beretta I brought.

Holstering it on my hip, I lean forward in the driver seat. Forearms on the wheel, getting a better view of the road.

If you want to kill anything, the fastest way is to cut off the head. Well here comes the animal now. In the back of a big maroon Lexus, tailed by a charcoal grey BMW 7-Series.

It's a lumpy old road. Narrow, with pot holes. You can't drive fast down here, and that's what I'm banking on.

I lean across the cabin and wind the passenger window all the way down. I wait until the Lexus is only metres away, then step on the accelerator.

The Volvo bolts out across the road and torpedoes the Lexus on the driver-side.

It's a heavy smash. I push the Lexus off the road and into the hedge.

The 7-Series swerves to a stop. I aim the shotgun through the open passenger window and let off a round. The shot punches through windscreen of the Beamer, the driver taking the hit.

A second later, the passenger door flies open. One of Dwyer's men rising out of the car.

I'm ready with another round. The guy's chest explodes.

He drops. I roll fast and low out of the Volvo. The car taking flak from the front passenger of the Lexus.

Tony B is armed with an automatic shooter. I hit the deck, drop the shotgun and draw the pistol from my hip. I aim under the floor of the Lexus and shoot the shins off the bastard. He falls to the ground. I stick a bullet in his forehead.

Meanwhile, the other Tony's door is stuck fast from the shunt. His seatbelt too. He struggles to get free, the same as Dwyer, his door mashed in by the Volvo.

Lenny's in the backseat too, under Dwyer's 'personal protection'.

First and last mistake. It makes this so much easier. Two dickheads, one stone.

But Lenny manages to slip out of the far side of the car. He wriggles his way through a hedgerow while I'm blowing the remaining Tony to pieces in the driver-seat.

I step onto the crumpled bonnet of the Volvo and hop down outside the rear passenger door.

I knock on the glass. "Alright?"

Dwyer knows he's not gonna outrun me. So he begs.

It's the usual script: How much money? What'll it take? Take twenty percent of my empire. No, make it thirty.

Fuck his empire. I slip another magazine in the Beretta, take aim and put a bullet through his right eye. I empty the rest of the clip into him--all the years of yes sir, no sir coming out.

Dwyer paints a pretty picture all over the beige leather of the Lexus.

I drop the empty pistol and grab the bag from the front passenger seat of the Volvo.

I step up onto the boot of the car. Then onto the roof. See Lenny limping across the field.

I jump over the hedge and land in the long, coarse grass. I sling the bag over a shoulder and run at a steady pace after Lenny.

The little prick looks over his shoulder. He draws a shooter of his own and lets off a couple of rounds.

But he's panicking. His aim all over the place. Being born into the Dwyer clan, he never had to do his own dirty work. All he did was point and shout and drink and fuck and piss on anyone he felt like.

I make up the ground and stop halfway across the field. Dropping the bag to the ground, I bring out my hunting rifle and take aim.

Lenny bounces around in the crosshairs, face a picture of fear. I wait for the right moment. For his head to line up nice. Then I pull the trigger.

There's a puff of blood from his head. He takes a nose-dive in the grass. I jog forward. Inspect the kill. Half of Lenny's skull missing.

I turn him over. Eyeballs frozen wide. Blood spatters up the side of his face. He looks innocent, like a kid.

Leaving him hidden in the grass, I jog back to the bag. I slip the rifle back inside, hook the bag over a shoulder and find a cut-through in the hedge.

I hurry back to the Volvo, picking up guns and cartridges. It all goes in the boot. But as I reach to close the lid, I realise I'm hit. A wound in the lower left side.

Blood seeps through my t-shirt. Don't know whose gun it came from. Must have been masked by the adrenaline. It's wearing off fast . . . thought something didn't feel right.

I slam the boot lid shut and get behind the wheel of the 940. The front-end is buggered, but it drives. I reverse clear of the wreckage and leave Dwyer and Lenny behind.

16

M ost of the time you grow up smarter and wiser. You learn what to do in life.

But sometimes, you had it figured out better when you were younger. When you were creative. You took chances. You threw yourself headlong into situations without overthinking.

There's a lot to be said for the carelessness of youth. So here's to my younger, crazier self. The lad who'd kick this barrel over with a boot. Who'd let the kerosene run all over the floor of the warehouse.

The daft bastard who'd take this match, strike it against the rough side of the box and toss it in the spill.

The wild child who'd watch a yellow-blue flame tear across the warehouse floor. And smile as it set fire to the hundreds of thousands of pounds' worth of supplies used to cut millions in street value cocaine.

The young devil who'd let the fire dance in his eyes before turning and walking out of a side door. Who'd stroll across the pitch-black car park, stepping over the body of an

Irish mafia foot-soldier as he bleeds out cold from the throat.

Who'd step through a gap in the fence and walk around the corner as the fire ripped through the roof and licked at the night air.

Who'd get back in his car and wait for the satisfying boom as the whole flammable mess explodes.

The old me who'd tell the stirring five-year old in the back seat it's just fireworks. And drive onto the next site on the list before the cry of the first fire engine.

Yeah, I've spent the past couple of years asking myself what Breaker would do and trying to do the opposite.

But right now, I'm putting all that on hold. I'm taking a holiday from my new improved self. The personal development seminars, the audiobooks, the should I, shouldn't I?

I'm letting Breaker do the talking. And right now he's in my ear, telling me Murphy has a cocaine lab to go with the warehouse. A big place. Industrial scale. Twenty-odd workers at a time, on twenty-four hour shifts.

When he hears about the warehouse, Murphy'll be expecting another hit straight after, during the night. So I sleep in the car, jacket zipped up and arms folded tight.

Ji-min sleeps wrapped up warm in her coat and a woolly white hat with a bobble on top, under the duvet from the apartment.

First thing in the morning, with the little one still snoozing. I peel myself out of the front passenger seat and get out of the car.

I roll my neck out and open the boot. I lift the floor panel and pull two SIG pistols from the space where the spare tyre should be.

I tuck both inside the pockets of my bomber jacket. You see, this is what you need to consider when you're buying a good coat. How big are the side pockets? Can you fit a pair of shooters in 'em?

I walk around the corner of a nondescript warehouse. It's a small industrial estate on the edge of town. The perfect place for a lab.

Swaying and staggering, I bounce off a wall and head towards a side door that's seen better licks of paint.

I sing a drunken tune. Hock up a mouthful of phlegm and spit it out. I sing louder. A football chant. I pound on the door and shout to be let in. That I need the toilet.

"I'll just piss right here then," I slur, undoing my fly.

I take a piss up against the wall, turning my face away from the spy hole in the door. But I hear movement behind.

I shake off as the lock opens on the door.

"Oi, fuck off nobhead," a doorman with a shotgun says.

I turn with my right-hand pistol drawn. Fire low into his gut. A second shot in the head.

He's down. I grab his shotgun and pump it.

Another man rounds the corner. I catch him cold with a shrapnel blast.

I push through a door. Up a flight of steel stairs, ditching the shotgun.

There's a couple more doors to get through. Then through a curtain of clear plastic flaps, guarding against contamination.

I stroll into the lab and pull out both pistols. I fire left and right. Enough to send the lab rats scurrying for the exits. It's a blur of illegal immigrants on a pittance of a wage. They're stripped to their undies with shower caps, masks and gloves their uniform. They run and shout, knocking over desks and lab equipment in their charge for the exits.

But I didn't bring the SIGs for them. I push through

another of those plastic curtains and find a pallet's worth of cocaine, wrapped in bricks and ready to go.

I unload most of my ammo into the pallets of coke. By the time I near the end of my clips, the room is clouded in a fine, white powdery mist. I slap a dusting of cocaine off my black jacket and move through the lab.

There's a pad and pen on a table with a recipe written down so the workers know how to cut the cocaine. I screw up the top sheet and write out a quick note for Murphy:

Call me if you want this to stop.

I scribble out a burner number and make a swift exit from the lab. Heading back to the car, I retrieve a spare clip from the boot.

I jam it in one of the SIGs, which I keep on me. Whamming the boot closed, Ji-min stirs in the backseat. I get behind the wheel and see her wake up, rubbing her eyes with white-mittened hands. Only her chubby red face visible over the blankets.

"I'm hungry," she yawns. "And bored."

"Bored? You've only been awake five seconds."

"What's for breakfast?" she asks.

"I've got one stop left to make," I say. "Then we'll get some brekkie and I'll take you to the park. You like pancakes?"

Ji-min breaks into a big smile, her head nodding like it's about to fall off.

"Right we are then," I say. "One more stop. There's a man I need to talk to."

The steel door shuts behind me with a bang. It sends a chill down my spine. But this time, I'm on the right side of the bars. The free side.

I shuffle inside the room with the other visitors and sit down on a chair halfway along six separate booths.

A pair of guards stand flat against the back wall. I nod at one. He recognises me. His name is Reg, a big black guy with a kind temperament. Which is rare in a shithole like this.

I turn to face the bulletproof divide. Most prisoners are let out into the adjoining room, where they'll sit across a table from their loved ones.

For the more dangerous or high profile guests of Strangeways, it's a black telephone receiver and inch-thick Plexiglass. The other inmates file out and engage in conversation with their families. There are smiles, tears, in some cases, strained or bored relations.

No such emotion in this booth. It's all about the hate.

Rudenko keeps me waiting before he appears. Dressed in the usual uniform of dark-blue jeans and a light-blue shirt, he's as fat and ugly as I remember. Maybe even more. He wears glasses and looks a decade older than when he went in. The small amount of hair left on his head turning white at the edges.

He freezes as he sees me on the other side of the glass. Hands in fists. Nostrils flaring. He finally steps forward and drops into his chair.

I pick up the receiver. Rudenko picks up his and holds it to his ear.

"Hello, Mr Rudenko."

"Hello Charlie," he says, in his thick Russian accent. "I see you're still alive."

"I am."

"Not for long," Rudenko says.

"Why, more clowns coming my way?"

Rudenko doesn't answer. He just stares. Stares like he's about to launch at the glass like an angry gorilla in a zoo.

"I've called in some guys from home," Rudenko says.

"Heavy hitters, huh?"

"Very heavy," Rudenko says. "Ex-Russian military."

"Thought you might."

"Which begs the question," Rudenko says. "Why are you sitting here in my prison?"

Rudenko is a picture of simmering rage. I wish I could film it. Bloody priceless.

But I get down to business. "I'm here to make you an offer, Mr Rudenko."

The old Russian squeezes the receiver in his hairy sausage fingers. He'd have made one hell of a powerlifter if he wasn't so fond of pizza and chips. "What could you possibly have to offer me, other than your head and your balls?"

"Connaugh Murphy," I say.

Rudenko's rage lifts an inch or two. Enough for him to see under the red mist. "What about him?"

"Turns out we've both got something in common," I say. "We both want him out of the picture."

"Last I heard, you were his little bitch," Rudenko says, turning his free hand into a yapping mutt. "You get tired of licking his balls?"

"Like I always told you and as I always told him, I'm like Switzerland. I'm neutral. This is a business offer, plain and simple."

"I don't do business with traitors," he growls.

I lean back in my chair. "You don't do much business at all is what I hear."

Rudenko grunts.

"You used to run over half of this city," I say. "Now you're down to selling knock-off goods and paying a handful of goons to defend a street corner . . . I'm guessing that's why you're bringing in those blokes from Russia. You're down to the bare bones. And it must be pretty expensive, staying on the right side of things in here."

Rudenko doesn't deny it.

"That pension pot's not gonna last forever," I say. "Neither's your reputation."

Rudenko shrugs. "Tell me something I don't know."

I lean in close to the glass. "What if you could take back all your old stomping grounds? And all Murphy's empire too?"

Rudenko doesn't say no. Which is as good as saying yes.

Yeah, I've got him now. If there's one thing that moves the Rudenko needle, it's money.

Money and power.

And if there's one person the old Russian wants to see eating worms more than me, it's his old nemesis, Connaugh Murphy.

As we eyeball each other through the glass, the cogs turn in Rudenko's head. He looks around. Shifts forward in his chair. "What are you proposing?"

"I take down Murphy . . . Him and his entire crew."

"That's a big crew," Rudenko says.

"Only the people who matter. The loyal. The well-paid. The rest will fall by the wayside. Or fight under a different flag when your boys step into the void."

Rudenko eyes me with suspicion. He's too paranoid to launch right into a free lunch.

"Think about it," I say, working him some more. "You can rebuild from the inside. And when you get out in two years— "

"Twelve months," Rudenko says, "reduced sentence."

"Well when you walk out of those big old iron gates in a year's time, you'll be back on the throne. The city will be yours. And I don't know whether you've been keeping tabs, but it's boom-time again. Murphy's making a killing on development deals alone. And while you're taking a shit in a seat-less pot, he's wiping his tanned arse with fifties . . . Your fifties."

"Two questions," Rudenko says. "Why do you want rid of Murphy? And why come to me?"

"One, he's protecting someone I want dead. Two, I can't go after Murphy if you're coming after me . . . Besides, I can't take him down on my own."

I leave Rudenko to mull it over.

"One minute," Reg yells behind me.

"Okay," Rudenko says. "I'll hold fire on you while you go after Murphy. But I'm not partnering up with a fucking traitor." He spits as he says the words. The spit lands on the glass between us.

"Say it, don't spray it," I say.

Rudenko leans in closer to the glass, his nose almost touching. He levels me with a cold stare. "I'll hold off my dogs for a few days. But after that . . ."

Rudenko doesn't say or do anything else. He doesn't need to. It's the same as a thumb across the throat.

"What was it you once said to me, Mr Rudenko? Something about pride being the enemy of profit?"

"Fuck you, dead man," Rudenko says with one last look of hatred. He drops the receiver and lets it swing. He disappears through a door.

I set the receiver down. Damn, I really thought I had him there.

"Visiting hours are over," Reg says as the room empties out.

I shake his hand. "Thank you officer."

Reg takes the fifty in my hand, payment for setting up the meet.

"Charlie," he nods, slipping the fifty in a pocket.

"Reg," I nod, on my way out.

Aﬀter pancakes with bacon and syrup, I take Ji-min to the park and push her on the swings.

It's a park I've never been to before, after an American-style diner I wouldn't normally frequent.

At times like this, you've gotta stay different and avoid anything familiar.

I give Ji-min a gentle shove, breathing in the smell of fresh cut grass. A light dew on the park. The seat wiped dry with the sleeve of my jacket.

"Higher!" Ji-min yells, with her trademark smile.

I wish I could smile as easy. Without the help of Rudenko, this is gonna be tricky. Gonna take some extra thinking time.

Time I haven't got.

"Higher, Uncle Charlie!"

I give Ji-min a hard shove. She flies into the air, little legs kicking.

"Too high!" she says, getting scared, the way Cassie used to get when I pretended I was gonna push her over the top,

As I slow the swing down and return it to a gentle rhythm, the phone in my pocket rings. A pre-paid mobile.

The same number I wrote on the sheet of paper in the cocaine lab.

Murphy's on the other end. "Fine, you win," he says. "Let's meet."

"I'll give you a time and place," I say.

"No," Murphy replies, his voice cold and charmless. "I'll tell you when and where."

"Fine, but bring Duffy," I say. "Or this process continues."

"Expect a text," Murphy says.

The line goes dead.

17

I 've got this little black book of contacts. Some of the names and numbers are no good anymore. But some still come in handy.

There are two. The first is Tommy.

Tommy works at a warehouse. It stocks thousands of items for a well-known online retailer, naming no names.

He drives fork lifts and wears a high-vis vest over his expanding waistline. Eats crisps for breakfast and sausage sandwiches for dinner and tea. Back when he could still fit through windows, he used to break into rich people's homes. Now he's gone straight and does a respectable bit of pilfering instead.

For a few quid, he'll lift you something off the stacks, then fiddle the paperwork. The warehouse is so big, you could see it from space, so no one notices.

Not when an item goes missing. And not when I park up in a loading bay outside a discreet side door.

Tommy appears, good to his word, a face full of ginger stubble. He sticks his head out of the door, looks both ways and carries an item covered in bubble wrap with just the head and the legs sticking out.

I hop out of the car and open the boot.

"Why the fuck do you want this?" he asks, pulling up his falling-down jeans.

"Why do you give a toss?" I answer, shoving a wad of money in his hand.

He counts it and nods, bumps my fist and waddles back in through the side door. He'll give Terry, the security guard, a slice for diverting the relevant security camera. In the meantime, I shut the boot and drive to my next stop. It's the other name in my book. A more serious player and a meeting in an underground car park. The kind without CCTV.

We leave our headlights on and our engines running. Piotr opens the rear of his silver Mitsubishi Shogun. A pair of suitcases sit side by side. One big, one a smaller travel-size.

He opens the big suitcase first. It's loaded with guns—pistols, a semi-automatic rifle and the necessary clips.

I pick up the weapons and check them over. I return them to inserts cut into a board of black foam.

Piotr unzips the small black travel case. There's a phone taped to an IED pipe bomb. He hands me a separate phone. Cheap and prepaid.

He's done well on short notice. I hand over the cash and lift the suitcases out of the boot. Piotr shuts the lid and runs a finger through the cash. He shakes my hand, happy with the count.

We exit the car park in opposite directions. I drive slow, avoiding speed bumps. Every lump in the road making my heart stop beating.

But I make it back to the apartments in one piece. I carry

the booster seat inside the entrance to the building and leave it in reception, hoping no one will nick it.

Returning to the apartment, Ji-min is right where I left her, watching a Disney film. I take a piss, grab a drink and when the film is over, sit her down on the side of the bed.

"Now I need you to listen to me carefully," I say, outlining the plan.

I put a smartphone down on the bedside table, along with a business card for a local cab firm. A firm that knows me. I tear the top sheet off a branded complimentary notepad and set it aside. I write out another address on the top sheet and tear it off. I tuck the address and cab firm card under the phone. But not before I've written out another note with instructions and a set phrase for Ji-min to say.

"Hopefully it won't be needed," I tell her. "But if I'm not back in four hours—and if you haven't heard from me—I want you to ring the number on the card. You know how to use the phone?"

"I'm not a baby," Ji-min says, like I'm stupid.

I set the timer on the phone to beep at the designated hour.

"When the phone beeps, you call the number and say '*I want a taxi from Big City Apartments Piccadilly*'. Can you say that?"

"Big City Apartments, Piccadilly," Ji-min says.

"Then you take the lift and press 'G'. When you get down to ground level, you wait inside the front door in reception. Come on, I'll show you."

I take Ji-min down in the lift and show her the button to press. On the ground floor, I carry the booster seat over to the front door. I leave it just inside.

"Push this green button," I say, pointing at the internal release. "The door will open on its own."

Ji-min loves pressing buttons. She reaches on her tiptoes and pushes the release. The door opens. Ji-min is thrilled with herself.

"But," I say. "Don't push the button until the taxi driver gets here. He'll walk to the door to get you. Then you push the button and tell him you need the booster seat. Got it?"

Ji-min nods.

"Let's practice," I say.

We pretend I'm the taxi driver. Ji-min loves it. Thinks it's a game. She hands me the address on a piece of paper, along with the money for the fare. We even pretend to get in a make-believe car.

When we're done, I change clothes and make us some cheese on toast. We eat together, then I leave her to play on the tablet, a juice and a chocolate bar left out on the side. The toilet light left on.

"You remember what to do?" I ask.

Ji-min nods. "Yes. But where are you going?"

"I've got some stuff to do," I say.

"Bad stuff?" Ji-min asks, like all this time she's seen right through me.

"Don't do anything I wouldn't do," I say, taking one last look at Ji-min. Even at such a young age, she's a dead ringer for her mum.

I pull the apartment door closed and head on out.

Manchester, 1998

The Happy Dragon's quiet and decked out in red and gold. Yunjin sits in the middle of the restaurant. She seems nervous. Checks her watch and sips on a glass of water.

I lurch across the floor of the Chinese restaurant, knocking into tables and chairs. Steadying myself. The waiting staff know me. They know this kind of world. They leave me be and let me approach the table. Yunjin goes to spring out of her seat.

I wave at her to stay put and drop into the seat opposite her, a hand to my side.

"You're hurt," Yunjin gasps.

"Only a bit," I say, reaching for a jug of table water.

Yunjin takes over, pouring me a glass. I down it in one. Cough and splutter. The gunshot wound on fire.

Yunjin's dessert arrives. A big slice of pineapple cake.

"I'll have what she's having," I say to Han, the waiter.

He's pencil thin and always polite. This is nothing he hasn't seen before, so he spins away without a word.

"What happened?" Yunjin asks.

"Better you don't know," I say. "But they won't be a problem anymore."

"Who?" Yunjin asks.

"Any of 'em," I say.

Han returns with a slice of cake.

"Cheers pal," I say, picking up a fork.

"You need hospital," Yunjin says.

"No hospital.".

"But you shot," she says.

I look down at the wound. "Yeah, I'd noticed."

"You not think right. You need help," Yunjin says.

"Not before I've had my cake," I reply, cutting a piece off with my fork. I scoop it in my mouth and savour it. "Shit that's good."

I swallow the cake and collapse sideways off the chair.

Yunjin hurries to my side. She presses her hands on my wound. "Call ambulance," she yells at Han.

"No," I say, a hand on her arm. "No hospital. No ambulance . . . They'll send you back to Korea. And they'll send me back to— "

That's the last thing about that I remember. That and the taste of pineapple cake.

19

I drive as far as my old lockup. The narrow, cobbled alley still the same. The lock a little rusty but after a fiddle with the key, the door opens to reveal my trusty old Volvo 940. The front end long since fixed up, the engine replaced and a new set of everything.

It was a bugger to find the parts, but I've fond memories of the old 940.

My first date with my ex-wife. The conception of my daughter. My liberation from the Dwyer family. And that's just to name a few.

I catch myself in a sentimental moment. *So many memories.* But I haven't got time for that. I whip the cover of it and transfer the stuff from the Peugeot. I leave the hire car parked outside the lockup and steer the Volvo along the cobbles.

The 940 handles like a dream. A bad dream where I'm fighting to steer an oil tanker down a white-water rapids. But the meet is only a short distance away.

Connaugh Murphy territory, down a dark, narrow street round the back of a derelict cotton mill. It's one of the few places they've yet to convert into flats and offices. I get there early and pull up halfway along the road, the brakes creaking.

I get out and roam around. Scope the place out. It's a road without cameras. Or witnesses. The perfect spot for a meeting. I check my watch, leave the engine running and turn the radio up. I get the old butterflies and imagine the look on Duffy's face when I've got my hands round his throat. I shake off the image. Check my watch. Stay focused, Charlie. They'll be here soon.

20

The meet was set. The boys ready.

Come alone and bring Duffy. That was the deal. The deal as this Cobb guy saw it.

Everyone knew the reputation. But reputations weren't bulletproof.

That's the way Ronnie Kerr saw it. He held up a fist as the lead Range Rover rolled to a stop. He spoke into the radio attached to his dark-blue shirt. "Wait for my signal."

Kerr got out of the Range Rover. He walked on ahead, soft steps up to a high red-brick wall. He peered around the corner and saw an old Volvo saloon parked halfway down the street, facing away from his position.

Cobb was waiting in the exact spot he'd been told. Expecting Murphy to roll into view at the opposite end of the street.

Kerr lifted his assault rifle to shoulder height. He looked through the zoom lens on the sighting and lined the back of the car up in his cross hairs.

Cobb was in the passenger seat. The exhaust kicking out fumes. The stereo playing out of an open driver window.

Kerr brought his radio to his mouth. "Target's in position. Green light all units."

He turned to see the rest of his six-man crew get out of the parked Range Rovers and shuffle over to his position. They moved as one, Duffy and Murphy nowhere to be seen.

Cobb was a fool. Blinded by his lust for revenge. Clearly, he had no idea who or what he was fucking with.

After all, things had changed since Cobb was last in town. Breaker was still an urban legend. But an old one, fading by the day. This was a different Manchester. And a different Murphy outfit. They'd raised their standards. Cobb was small-time now. And Kerr had always considered him overhyped in the first place.

Well finally Murphy had seen sense. Cobb was a relic from a bygone era. A thorn in everyone's side. It was time to put the old nag down and bury the name Breaker under a thousand tonnes of newly-poured concrete.

Kerr waved his men on. They approached fast and quiet, splitting in two groups of three.

Cobb must have seen them in his mirrors. But even he wasn't stupid enough to make a move now. Not with half a dozen armed men advancing on his position.

Kerr spoke into his radio. "If he moves, take him down. Otherwise, I get the fucking kill."

They came up on the car and slowed their pace, Kerr controlling the assault team with a series of hand movements.

He crept up to the driver-side window. Engine ticking over. A song drifting out of the window. Neil fucking Diamond, *"I am... I said"*.

"What's this shit?" one of the men asked.

"Quiet," Kerr said. "Moving in."

Kerr got behind his rifle sight and paused. Still Cobb

didn't move. Maybe he was waiting for the right time, a weapon on his lap. Well he wouldn't get the chance.

Kerr whirled around to take aim. Yet he hesitated, rifle sight dropping. He exchanged confused glances with his man on the opposite side of the car.

"What the fuck?" Kerr said, staring at the mannequin sitting behind the wheel.

It sat dressed in dark clothing under a black wig. And Kerr noticed a cheap silver handset in the mannequin's hand. It started to ring. He reached inside the car and picked up the phone.

Kerr answered the call.

"Christ, Ronnie," Cobb said on the other end of the line. "Still playing army?"

"What is this?" Kerr said. "Where are you?"

"Behind you," Cobb said.

Kerr spun, rifle at the ready. All he saw was a wall. But more than a wall.

A wall with a small camera stuck to it seven feet up.

"Say cheese, Ronnie."

Kerr turned back to the car. Another beeping sound. A second phone. Screen lighting up blue through a white t-shirt worn by the mannequin. It was strapped and wired to a pipe.

"Say bye, Ronnie."

Kerr dropped the phone from his ear. *"No— "*

I watch the pipe bomb explode in all directions. All six of Murphy's assault team taken down. The video feed on my tablet turns to static.

Shame about the Volvo. Like I said, so many memories. I drop the prepaid phone and crunch it under my boot.

Murphy tried to screw me, just as I thought.

I leave the tablet in the boot and pull the Heckler & Koch assault rifle from the big suitcase.

I holster a pistol on my hip and another by my ribs. I tap my knuckles against my Kevlar vest for luck and zip up my black jacket over the top.

Hanging the rifle strap over my shoulders, I shut the boot and go to climb back inside the Peugeot. It's parked by the side of a B-road leading into the heart of Wheatley Village. Only a half-mile drive from here.

But I freeze as a black Range Rover comes up the road.

It speeds towards me and brakes heavy to a stop. I hold the rifle down by my side, finger on the trigger.

The front doors open on the Range Rover. A rear door too, near side.

Three men get out. They're armed, much the same as me. And I'm outnumbered.

"You Cobb?" one of 'em asks in a Russian accent. He's a pale-skinned guy with shaved white hair. He's middle-aged. The other pair in their early forties. Guy number two with shaggy brown hair and a square face. Guy number three darker skinned with black hair and eyebrows that won't take a day off.

They're battle-hardened bastards. I can tell.

"Yeah, I'm Cobb," I say.

"Our employer said you could use a hand."

"Your employer was right." I take my finger from the rifle trigger and step forward. "Charlie," I say, offering a hand.

The bald guy takes it. A stiff handshake. "Oleg." He points at his two pals. "This is Dragan," he says of the shaggy-haired guy, "and this is Vitaly."

We shake hands.

"So what's happening?" Oleg asks.

I look along the road. "It's a half mile into the village. Beyond that, there's a country mansion. It'll be guarded. But I lured the best of his security away. They won't be coming back."

"And the plan of attack?" Dragon asks.

"Attack," I shrug.

Oleg and the boys smile.

Murphy's country pile is a ten-acre estate tucked away in the Cheshire village of Wheatley. The place is hidden away behind high stone walls and tall wooden gates.

I've been here before, on business. The biggest place you've ever seen. Posher than plums in Prince Charles' mouth. But close enough to the city to attend to all Murphy's dirty deeds.

Now this is no time for subtlety. And let's face it, subtlety's not my strong suit. So we sweep through the village at speed, me in front, the Range Rover close behind.

We flash past the Post Office. The bakery. The chippy and the local corner shop. Past the Black Sheep Inn and the entrance to the farm shop and onto a lane marked *'Private'*.

A lane that runs a half mile to the perimeter of Murphy's home base.

From what I remember, he wouldn't normally have a twenty-four-seven guard patrolling the walls. But there's nothing normal about today.

Today, you can guarantee he'll be tooled up and ready. Murphy's a smart operator, after all. Nothing complacent about the guy. He'll be in there with Duffy, waiting on a call from Kerr. A confirmation of the kill. And his next move to order them to track down Ji-min. To wrap up the whole bloody mess in a pretty pink bow.

Well sorry old pal, but here we bloody come.

The Range Rover pulls up alongside me. It's on Rudenko's coin, so who cares if the front end gets smashed to shit.

Oleg is at the wheel. The other two with their windows down, assault rifles at the ready.

Oleg accelerates past. I tuck in behind. He speeds up as we near the front gates. The Range Rover blasts right on through, the wooden gates splintering like they're made of toothpicks.

As Dragan and Vitaly exchange fire with a pair of guards, I pull up sharp and jump out.

We fan and move up the sweeping green lawns that rise towards the mansion either side of the driveway. The house is even bigger than I remember, painted cream with a slate roof and giant windows.

I expect more guys to come piling out of the front doors, but they emerge from down the sides, using the walls as cover.

We're expose, so I drop to the turf. A small target and trade fire, turf exploding in front of me.

I glance over my shoulder. Dragan is using a large boulder for protection. Vitaly staying wide, in the trees on the far side of the property.

Where the fuck is Oleg?

I hear the roar of a v12 engine. The Range Rover barrelling up the lawn. Oleg leans on the horn. I roll out of the way, the front passenger tyre missing me by an inch.

Oleg bails at the last. The Range Rover takes a beating of shrapnel, but makes it to the house.

Battered and bruised, it ploughs into a giant fishbowl of a window at the front of the mansion.

Glass and stone explode. I'm up on my feet, peppered by raining debris.

In the wake of the distraction, we get the better of Murphy's men. We hit 'em from all angles with semi-automatic shots to the chest and head.

Rudenko's boys are experienced pros and good marksmen used to a gunfight. We fold in together as one unit, slick as oiled seagulls. As if we've been working together for years.

We step through the hole created by the Range Rover, into a vast living room with modern furniture. Everything is bright and white. A giant L-shaped sofa and French windows look out over a terrace.

But there's more resistance to come. And it comes running into the living room, a pair of guards dressed smart in black suits. But we're waiting for 'em, taking cover behind the smoking grill of the Range Rover.

We rest our elbows on the hot, crumpled metal and take aim. It's a firing squad. They're down before they even see us. And seconds later, we're moving into the hallway.

We split up. Sweep the other rooms. I hear a crack of gunfire. A body dropping.

Oleg returns. His two pals close behind. I meet them in the grand hallway. A double staircase rising and merging in a single balcony above.

The hallway is carpeted thick and white. The stairs too. Not great for getting the blood out, but good for shuffling up fast and quiet. We split in pairs and take either staircase. Me and Oleg leading the way.

We meet at the top. I hear voices. One of 'em's Murphy's. The other I don't recognise. Mancunian, but muffled behind a door at the end of the hall.

I nod to the others. We move fast and take our positions outside the door.

I test the nob. It turns. I fling the door inward and we pile through the doorway, into a large home office.

The place is decked out with antique leather chairs, a big oak desk in front of a giant portrait of Murphy.

The man himself freezes, stood over his desk, phone in hand. Duffy's here too. Backing up against the wood-panelled wall to my left.

"If you're calling Kerr, don't bother," I say. "He can't hear you from the afterlife."

Murphy hangs up the phone. "He's yours," he says, glancing at Duffy. "Take him."

"We will," I say.

"And me?" Murphy asks, hand close to a pistol lying prone on his desk.

"You shouldn't have screwed me over," I say.

Duffy edges along the wall.

"Come on, Charlie," Murphy replies. "I'm sure we can come to some kind of arrangement."

"Well that's up to my associates here." I turn to the Russians. "What do you say, lads?"

"We're happy to discuss," Oleg says with a smile.

Murphy cottons on fast. I see the panic in his eyes. For once he looks something other than in control. He ages ten years in three seconds, trembling, fumbling, broken.

Oleg takes a step forward. Murphy backs away from his desk.

I turn my attention to Duffy. But too late. There's a secret exit in the wall. A door that looks like any other panel. Duffy pushes through it and disappears.

I leave Murphy negotiating for his life. Promises of money, power, a slice. Doubling and tripling their fee.

It's none of my business now. I'm laser-focused on what I came for.

The bastard's ahead of me, running down the stairs. I bound down the other staircase and cut off his nearest exit.

He stops and swerves me, out through the back. I chase him through to an enormous country kitchen.

The kitchen leads out to a large courtyard flanked by a stables to the right and an open garage to the left. My boots crunch over light gravel as I give chase towards the stables.

Duffy disappears through the stable door. I realise my rifle is empty and ditch it on the ground.

Treading slow to the door, I ease it open. It creaks. I half expect a bullet or a fist. I didn't see a gun in Duffy's jeans, but you've got to expect the worst.

Horses whinny and snort inside the gloom of the stables. Unsettled by a stranger.

I bend low and check under each stable door, looking for the presence of human feet. But there's only a pair of four-legged creatures inside. One white and the other chest-nut-brown.

The place stinks of hay and manure. Or maybe it's just the smell of Duffy. I push out through the door at the opposite end of the stables and round the building, pistol in hand.

There's still no sign of Duffy. So I head to the garage—a cream Bentley Continental and bright-green Lamborghini parked nose-first to the courtyard.

I look around me. *Where the hell is he?*

Then comes the answer. Headlights on. The rasp of a supercar engine.

The green Lamborghini accelerates out of the garage. It's too late to dive out of the way. So I take a hit and find myself on the bonnet with Duffy behind the wheel.

I hold onto an air vent, raise my pistol and open fire through the windscreen. The Lamborghini pulls off the driveway and onto the lawn. It skids one-eighty to a stop, spraying mud and turf.

The sudden stop sends me flying off the bonnet. I roll on the soft grass and onto my feet.

Duffy spills out of the driver seat, onto the lawn. He picks himself up, clutching a bleeding shoulder.

He scrambles away from me, but I'm on him in a few strides. I tuck the pistol away.

Duffy turns to fight me. Throws a punch. I take it on the chin. It's nothing. I grab him by the lapels. Hit him once. He's dizzy on his feet. A right to the jaw puts him down on his back.

As he rolls onto his front, I notice Duffy isn't carrying. The prick thought he was untouchable.

Everyone's touchable.

I roll him over with a boot. "Why?" I ask.

"Why what?" Duffy asks, spitting grass from his mouth.

I kneel low over him and whip out my gun. "Why the woman? Why her?"

"'Cause I saw her. 'Cause I wanted to. 'Cause I hate fucking chinks. All of the fucking above. What do you fucking care?" Duffy knows he's dead. And he's talking like it. "Get it over with," he says. "Put a bullet in me."

I look at the pistol. Toss it aside. I pull a large hunting knife from a sheath on my belt.

"If I could, I'd make this last all week," I say. "But seeing as we're on a tight schedule, I'll just have to settle for a few minutes of entertainment."

Duffy looks at the blade. His breathing shortens.

"It's not your way," Duffy says, unsure of himself.

"Really?" I say. "You know my name?"

"Yeah, it's Cobb," he sneers.

"No, my other name."

He doesn't want to say it. Doesn't need to.

I pause with the knife and wonder if this is going against every change I've been trying to make to myself. If this is Yunjin would have wanted. What Cassie would say. What Jimin would think.

But we're past that now. And let's face it, I'm not one of life's nice guys, no matter how you dress me up.

And who knows, maybe the world needs guys like me, to stop guys like this.

All this time I've been pretending I'm different to the Murphy's and the Rudenko's.

But I'm not. I'm one of 'em. Maybe the worst of 'em. The man who gives the nightmares nightmares.

The universe must maintain a balance. That's what I've been reading in all these self-help books. That it must match energies like for like. And that the universe goes about its business through us, using each of us as instruments to express itself.

If that's true, then maybe this is my calling. Maybe I'm an instrument for the universe. An instrument of karma matching every murderous scumbag act with a like energy in return.

Well, I'll try my best.

First I stick the knife inside Duffy's groin. I slice across, cutting open his ball-sack. He screams like nothing I've ever heard before.

I take out the knife and slip it in the soft flesh of his gut. I drag the blade upwards.

It's like descaling a fish. His screams travel far over the wide open spaces of Murphy's private estate.

Duffy's guts spill out. I stop at the breastbone. Prise out the knife and slash his throat. He chokes on the blood, hands to his neck. I let him splutter a little longer, watching the pain and suffering in his eyes.

"Yunjin says hello," I tell him, thrusting the knife deep into his heart.

It's a killer blow, his jaw open, eyes locked in terror and mouth like an overflowing well, pooling and cascading with blood. I leave the knife standing in his heart, only the handle visible.

I step over Duffy's body and don't give him a second look. The Lamborghini is dug into the lawn, its engine smoking. It catches fire. I leave it to burn, returning to the house.

I enter through a sliding glass door left open. It runs along the side of an indoor swimming pool, as swish as hell. There's a glass ceiling and a hot tub at the far end.

Murphy floats face-down in the pool, dark blood staining the light-blue shimmering water.

I go looking for the others and find Oleg in the kitchen. He has his head in a built-in, American-style fridge, his rifle on the granite top of a kitchen island next to two large leather holdalls with the zips open. The holdalls are full to the brim with stacks of cash. There must be a million, easy.

"Where's the cash from?" I ask.

"Murphy was kind enough to show us inside his safe," Oleg replies, his head still in the fridge.

"Right, well, let's go," I say. "The villagers will have heard the gunfire."

"No," Oleg says, taking an oversized chicken leg from the fridge. He bites into it.

"What do you mean, no?"

Oleg turns and leans an arm on the fridge door. "The job isn't finished,"

I realise too late and hear footsteps behind me. Dragan and Vitaly.

Oleg drops his chicken leg.

As Dragan slips a length of garrotte over my head, I get a hand between the wire and my throat.

Meanwhile, Oleg pulls a knife. I kick the fridge door shut. It slams against his hand, forcing the blade from his grip. I spin Dragan around and punch Vitaly in the jaw. He falls through a glass door, his pistol spilling across the kitchen floor.

As Dragan pulls harder on the wire, I slam him against the counter behind us. But he holds on tight as Oleg shakes the pain from his hand and bends over to pick up the knife.

I boot the fridge door again. Oleg's head is caught between door and steel frame. He falls forward into shelves stuffed with food, bottles and jars smashing all over the floor.

Vitaly lurches back up, daggers of glass sticking out of his face. He stoops for his gun, so I grab a heavy black wok off a hook on the wall. Vitaly catches my arm and knocks the pan from my hand. He punches me in the guts. Pulls a meat knife from a block and slashes like a maniac.

I twist and turn out of the way. Dragan takes the end of the cleaver in the back.

As he cries in pain, I reach behind me, pull the knife from Dragan's back and lodge it in the side of Vitaly's head.

He slaps to the kitchen floor next to Oleg, who's on all fours.

He retrieves his knife and cuts me just above the knee. I almost fall. Dragan holds on, the wire cutting deeper into my hand.

I can't keep this up forever, so I force Dragan over to the Range cooker. It's a big silver Aga with black gas hobs on top.

I struggle to turn the rear right knob, fingers slippy with blood and Oleg getting to his feet.

I flick on the knob, hear the gas and pull Dragan down with me—our faces on the plates.

Dragan tries to pull us back up. I fight to hold us down, stretching to reach the spark switch as Oleg staggers towards us.

My finger slips off the switch. Once, twice, but the third time I get it. There's a spark. The rush of a flame. Dragan screaming. The wire releasing. I push away from Dragan, his face and hair on fire. He lurches to the sink to douse the flames. The smell of cooking flesh in the air.

That leaves Oleg blocking my path with the knife. I'm down to one hand. The other cut to ribbons. Yet he backs up towards the counter.

Is he letting me go?

No, trading his knife for his rifle. I'm out of time, out of weapons, out of options. Officially goosed.

Oleg takes aim. There's a gun shot. But not from the Russian's gun.

His eyes go blank. He falls forward, a face-dive to the floor. A hole in the back of his skull.

Lisa stands in the open doorway out to the courtyard.

Dressed in jeans, sandy-coloured jacket and riding boots. The pistol in her hand smokes. She fires again. I think it's for me. But it's for Dragan, turning from the sink, his hair wet and face frazzled. He collapses to the seat of his arse.

I raise my hands, at her mercy. From what I know of Lisa, she doesn't have any.

In the meantime, Dragan left the kitchen tap running.

I motion to it. "Before you do it, do you mind if I turn the tap off?"

"You got OCD or something?" Lisa asks.

"I hate wasting water," I say. "I'd feel better if, you know . . ."

Yet she lowers her weapon and steps into the kitchen. "Relax, the gun's for them, not you."

I breathe a sigh of relief and move to the sink. I turn off the tap.

"Thanks for saving me," I say.

"Don't flatter yourself," Lisa replies. "I don't want Rudenko's men chasing me halfway across the country."

"And what about me?" I ask.

"You?" Lisa laughs. "You're harmless."

"And you're not sore over Murphy?" I ask.

Lisa shakes her head. "What Duffy did to that woman . . . They both had it coming."

She snatches a key fob from a bowl on the kitchen table, heaves a bag of money off the counter and backs out of the kitchen door.

Lisa disappears from view. I cradle my bleeding hand and hobble tired as far as the doorway, trying not to slip on the blood. As I emerge into the courtyard, there's a deep rumble. The growl of a six-litre engine.

Lisa pulls out of the garage in the Bentley. She rolls by

me with her window down. She blows me a kiss and flashes me a smile, just to wind me up.

I watch her cruise down the driveway in the Bentley, steering around bodies. She accelerates through the smashed front gates and opens it up along the lane.

I double-back into the kitchen, grab the second bag of money and limp down the driveway as far as the Peugeot.

Climbing inside, I drag my right leg in with me and place my foot on the accelerator pedal. I pull the driver door shut, make a three-point turn and drive away through the gates, leaving a bloodbath in my wake.

I make it through the village and out onto the B-road, steering and changing gear with my one good hand.

Cold and dizzy, everything hurts except the cut on my leg. Which isn't a great sign. But I should be okay. I should make it.

Yet I wonder what I'll do when I do make it. The vet I used to use emigrated a couple of years ago. The hospital is out. And the only doctor I know who'll take a backhander isn't answering his phone.

I toss the burner onto the passenger seat, realising there's a bigger problem. The Peugeot lurches, coughs, stalls. Freewheels to a stop by the side of the road, a burning smell inside the cabin.

The brakes don't respond. The Peugeot rolls into a ditch in a wild meadow.

I open the door and fall out into the long, wild grass and heather. As I struggle to my feet, I see the problem. Bullet holes in the bodywork. An undercarriage leaking oil. And a busted radiator steaming through the vents on the bonnet.

The Peugeot is toast. The deposit shot to shit. I should have paid for the full cover, but who pays for that, right?

I limp round to the passenger side and open the door. I

take out the bag of money and hook it over my shoulder. I scramble up the bank, dragging my right leg behind me.

Straightening up, I set off down the road, limping like a zombie the day after the apocalypse.

I start to tire. Stop to throw up. Keep limping. As long as it takes.

But it's no good. I'm not gonna make it.

I drop the money. Try and shed a bit of weight. Yeah, that's better. I make it another couple of feet, then collapse.

I don't even feel the fall. I roll onto my side and watch the grass blow in the breeze. So tired.

So, so tired.

anchester, 1998

I wake up in the back of the restaurant, flat out on a steel table. Han and a couple of other waiting staff stand over me.

"What happened?" I ask, feeling a pinch in my side.

"I train as nurse," Yunjin says. "For few months."

I look to my left. There's a rice bowl on the counter. Inside the bowl, a spent bullet covered in my blood.

"You're a natural," I say, feeling the stitching around my wound.

"I stop the bleeding, but you need doctor. It might be infected— "

"I'll be alright," I say lurching upright, a hand to my side.

The stitching hurts like a fucker. I swing my legs over the edge of the table. Yunjin steadies me, a hand on my shoulder.

"What we do now?" she asks. "Where we go?"

"Wherever you want," I say. "It's over."

"Your boss?"

"You won't be hearing from him anymore." I shift onto

my feet and pull my t-shirt over my head, fighting through the agony.

I open my wallet and take out a wad of notes. I slip 'em to Han. "For the trouble."

Han nods. He's a good guy. He offers me the rice bowl with the bullet in. *"Souvenir?"*

I laugh. First time in ages. Does it always hurt?

I tell Han to keep it and we leave the restaurant. I drive the Volvo to the lockup. It's a miracle we're not pulled over, what with all the damage to the car.

I switch the 940 with the Calibra and return to the flat with Yunjin. I pull on the washing machine. She fusses. I swat her away and drag the machine out a couple of feet.

I peel the bin bag off the wall and push the machine back in its place. I hand the bag to Yunjin. "Here."

"No, I can't," she says.

I grab her wrist, open her palm and shove the bag in her hand. "Enough to get you started."

I don't take no for an answer. And I don't let her take the bus either. I drive her home in the Calibra.

"You still need doctor," Yunjin says.

"I know a guy," I say. "I'm on my way there."

"And after that, what you do?"

I shrug. "Go to the chippy. Watch some telly."

"No, for money."

"I'll figure something out. You?"

"Same," Yunjin says. "Keep in touch?"

"Sure," I say. "We've got each other's numbers."

She gets out. Sticks her head back in the car. "I make you Korean food. Next week. Fried cockroach."

I pull my face, feeling queasy.

She laughs. "It's joke. I'm great cook. You like it."

I smile and nod, watch her step inside and drive away.

I head straight to the vet. He runs a secret practice out of the back of his surgery. Cash in hand only from two-legged patients who need more than a flea injection.

The vet checks me out. Tells me the wound isn't infected. That Yunjin did a good job. It'll heal up nice.

I buy some illegal painkillers off him and return home. Go the chippy. Watch the telly. Get some kip.

A couple of days later, I'm moving around better. Not up to a run yet, but a walk to the shops. I buy a paper, bog roll and a Milkybar.

As I'm walking with my shopping towards the tower block estate, a car pulls up alongside me. A dark-blue Bentley no less. The rear window whirs down. I peer inside.

I recognise the face. It's a guy called Connaugh Murphy. Jet-black hair swept back with the first specks of grey. He's always well turned out. Today, in a silver suit and thin black tie. "Charlie," he says in his mock-posh accent, like he comes from a better class of gutter. "You know who I am?"

I shrug.

"The name's Murphy. You can call me Mr Murphy . . . Some feat you pulled off the other day. It's earned you quite the reputation."

"Don't know what you're on about," I say.

"No, course you don't," Murphy smiles. "Still, you must be looking for something to do now the old bastard Dwyer's in the ground."

"This a job offer?"

"Not a job offer, Charlie. An opportunity."

"Oh yeah?"

"To join a growing organisation. About to grow even faster now Dwyer's out of the picture."

"In what capacity?"

"Any you like," Murphy says. "Apart from the top job, of course."

"Sorry, Mr Murphy. I don't work for families no more."

"Oh no?"

"No, I'm freelance now."

Murphy plays with the rim of the hat perched on his knee. "But you *are* for hire."

"Yeah, but neutral," I say. "Like that country . . ."

"Switzerland," Murphy says.

"Yeah, that's it," I say. "Switzerland."

"Right you are then," Murphy replies. "I'll be in touch."

The window winds up and the Bentley pulls away from the kerb. I take another bite of my Milkybar and watch it cruise away.

22

Ji-min was halfway through her Kinder Chocolate bar when the phone beeped on the bedside table. She turned off the kids channel she'd found on the TV and slid down off the bed. She folded the wrapper over the half-eaten chocolate bar and tucked it in her jeans pocket. Next, Ji-min picked up her coat and pulled it on.

She saw three notes left on the table, along with the business card for the taxi company. One of the notes was screwed up. She unfolded it and lay it flat on the table.

With Mr Moo in hand, Ji-min picked up the phone and pushed the blue 'call' button in the shape of a telephone. And then the last call made, labelled 'Taxi'.

She picked up the note with the instructions on what to say to the woman on the end of the call. She looked at Mr Moo. He whispered to her in Korean. She whispered back. It was the way they always talked. They nodded at one another—Ji-min agreed, it was a good idea.

"Big City Apartments, Piccadilly," she said when the

woman answered her call. "Going to . . ." Ji-min read out the address on the piece of paper and gave her Uncle Charlie's name.

The woman recognised the name. "Ah, yes, Mr Cobb. That's fine, love. The taxi will be there in ten minutes."

Ji-min put down the phone and gathered what she needed, stuffing Mr Moo in her coat pocket. She went to the toilet, like you were supposed to before things like cinema trips and car journeys. "Go now or forever hold your pee," her mum used to say.

Ji-min washed and dried her hands, zipped up her coat and left the apartment. As the door clicked shut behind her, she walked to the lift and pushed the button for down.

The lift arrived and opened. Ji-min stepped inside and pushed the button for the ground floor - the big green button with 'G' on it.

Ji-min liked the lift. And it was a real thrill riding it on her own. It made her feel grown-up, like one of the adults.

The lift opened. She walked across reception and stood inside the doorway for the taxi man.

After a few minutes, a car pulled up on the street. It had the same logo as the business card her Uncle Charlie had left for her.

A man got out. Old like Uncle Charlie, with a dark-blue baseball cap and a greying beard. He was Asian, like her. But from a different part of Asia. The Middle East, her mum said they called it.

He was slim and friendly. Waving to her from the other side of the glass. Ji-min stretched on her tiptoes and pressed the release button for the door.

The taxi driver pushed open the glass door and sized her up.

"Ji-min, is it?" he asked in a foreign-sounding Mancunian accent. He looked at the booster seat. "And this must be for you."

Ji-min nodded. She took out one of the pieces of notepaper and handed it to the taxi man.

"I'm Farhad," the man said. "This where we're going?"

"Yes please," Ji-min said, taking out the money her Uncle Charlie had left her.

Farhad checked the money. He raised an eyebrow. "Not like Charlie to miscount. Are you sure this is all he gave you?"

Ji-min nodded.

"I'm sorry, but I don't think this'll be enough to cover the trip."

Ji-min's face fell in disappointment. *"Oh."*

Farhad looked at her, shrugged and tucked the money away in a chest pocket on the front of his crumpled white shirt. "Tell you what, we'll square it some other time."

"What does square it mean?" Ji-min asked, as Farhad carried the booster seat to the car.

He fixed it tight to the backseat and stepped aside as Ji-min climbed up into the seat.

"It means, we'll sort it out later," Farhad explained, fastening Ji-min into the booster seat. "It's just something people say."

"Why do people say it?" Ji-min asked, as Farhad started the engine and pulled on his seatbelt.

'Because people say one thing when they mean something else," he continued, indicating to pull out.

"Why?"

"They just do," Farhad said.

"Oh," Ji-min sighed.

As Farhad nudged out into a busy flow of traffic coming from the train station, she looked around her. "This car is big."

"Fairly big, yeah," Farhad said, squeezing out into a gap.

"Why is it big?" Ji-min asked, as the journey begun.

23

I hear a car coming in the distance. Either it's gonna run me over, the driver's gonna call the police, or they'll stop and call an ambulance. Neither one of them is gonna do me any favours. The best thing they can do is ignore me altogether. Or stop and take the money. What do I care? Not like I can spend it in the morgue or in a prison cell. Whichever comes first.

At the rate I'm bleeding, the safe money's on the slab.

Oleg knew what he was doing with that knife. My biology isn't the best. Not when I'm close to passing out. But I think he may have severed an artery. A main vein for sure.

I try and lift my head to get a better look. Maybe I can apply a better tourniquet than the belt from my jeans. But as I try and sit up on the road, all I feel is dizzy.

I flop back to the tarmac. Bag of cash by my side. Trail of blood along the road. A crow crowing in the neighbouring field. And the tyres of that car rushing towards me.

This must be what a hedgehog feels like. Or a squashed rabbit.

Except the car is slowing to a stop. As I turn my head, I

see tyres. A number plate. A silver grill. A pair of feet get out of the car. Jeans and scruffy trainers. They hurry to my side.

"Charlie, bloody hell."

I know that voice. Who is that? A face looks over me from under a dark-blue baseball cap.

"Farhad?"

"Shit, Charlie mate. What are you doing out here?"

"What am I—? Just get me out of here."

Farhad grabs me by the collars. He's a spry bloke and stronger than he looks. He helps me to my feet and supports my weight.

"The bag, too," I wheeze.

Farhad heaves the bag of money over a shoulder and slow-walks me to his cab. I almost collapse. Almost take him with me. But he fights to steady me. I find some strength in my legs and grab hold of the roof of the car.

Farhad opens a rear passenger door and eases me onto the backseat. He drops the bag of money on my lap and slams the door shut.

As he runs around the car to the driver-side door, I look to my right.

Ji-min sits in her booster seat eating the remains of a chocolate bar, half of it on her face.

"What the—?" I struggle to stay conscious.

"What's all that red?" Ji-min asks me.

"Uh," what a question when you're bleeding out. "It's ketchup," I say.

"That's a lot of ketchup."

"Never mind that," I say. "What the hell are you doing here?"

Ji-min puts a hand on my shoulder like I'm stupid. "We're protecting you."

"We?"

"Me and Mr Moo." Ji-min makes the stuffed cow's head nod in agreement. The girl's even more bonkers than me.

In the meanwhile, Farhad settles in behind the wheel. He pulls the taxi to the right and spins the car round in the road.

I'm already low in my seat. But I slide lower as police cars flash by on the way to the village.

I look around me. "I hope you know a good valet."

"Don't worry about that," Farhad says. "Where to?"

"Anywhere but here," I say.

"Is there a doctor? A hospital?" he continues.

"Anywhere but there," I reply.

"We've got to get you somewhere, mate. You're a bloody mess."

"Tell me about it," I say, trying to think through my options.

Hell, trying to think.

Ji-min holds Mr Moo to her ear. She whispers something to herself in Korean and nods. She takes a slip of note paper from inside a coat pocket. "Here," she says, holding it out for Farhad. "This is where."

Farhad contorts an arm to snatch the paper from Ji-min's hand.

"What's that?" I ask of the slip of paper.

"The address you gave me," Ji-min says, like it's obvious.

I'm struggling to compute. Until I notice another piece of notepaper on the central console of the dash.

Ji-min gave Farhad the wrong address on purpose. That's why they were on the way there, to pick me up. She worked out the whole bloody thing.

"Is this right, Charlie?" Farhad asks, still holding the slip of paper.

"Yeah, it's right."

I look across at Ji-min, not knowing whether to laugh or cry. "Your mum was right. You are a little genius."

Ji-min nods. *"Mm."* She stuffs the end of her chocolate bar in her mouth and looks at me. "Uncle Charlie, w*hy* are you covered in ketchup?"

Lucky for me, I pass out.

I remember flashes: Coming to in the back of the cab. Handing Farhad a stack of notes for the fare, the blood and the trouble.

Then I remember the old front door. It used to be black. But they painted it green.

And the house. It looks different. New furniture, new beige carpet. They knocked through a wall.

I remember newspaper on the kitchen floor. A brand new kitchen table. Rectangle rather than a circle. An extender, with four chairs cleared out of the way.

That's about all I remember. Aside from faces. Blurred, tanned faces and voices. *Women.*

Then a laptop. My belt removed. A debate over what to do

Towels and water fetched. The sting of antiseptic. A needle sticking out of my leg and not feeling a thing.

Now I see my ex-wife, Mandy and daughter, Cassie. Are they real?

With my condition, there's no guarantee. They fuss over me. Mandy working a needle and thread.

Maybe it's all part of the same dream. Yunjin, Ji-min, Murphy . . . Am I back in New York, sleeping between shifts?

I drift off again. Then everything sharpens. I'm back in my body, anchored by pain. The world coming into focus.

I'm in the kitchen of the family home, on the dining table by the window. It's hard. Sturdy. Nice bit of wood . . . When did they get this?

"Is this pine?" I ask.

"Beech," Mandy says. "Ikea."

"How was your holiday?" I ask.

"Wonderful," Mandy says. "Sun, sand, cock—"

"Ugh, I don't wanna hear."

"Tails," Mandy says with a scowl. "Cock-tails."

"Uh, sorry. I'm still not thinking right."

Mandy dries her hands on a towel. "When did you ever?"

"Your bedside manner could do with some work," I say, lifting my head and inspecting the stitches. "Even if your needlework is pretty damn good."

"It ought to be," Mandy says. "I fixed you up enough times. Plus, we've got Google now." Mandy sighs and shakes her head. "What have you gotten into now, Charlie?"

"Nothing that's gonna crawl back out of its grave."

"Well that's a relief," Mandy says, taking out an e-cigarette. She takes a puff on it. The air smelling of strawberries.

"I thought you quit," I say, sitting up.

"I did," Mandy says. "It's called vaping. It's harmless."

"Harmless except for all the chemicals in it."

"I'll be fine," Mandy says.

"It's not you I'm worried about."

"Oh, thanks," Mandy says, rolling her eyes. "Next time I'll let you bleed to death."

"Just not in front of the girls," I say.

Right on cue, Cassie and Ji-min appear hand-in-hand in the kitchen.

"Dad!" Cassie says, throwing her arms around me. It hurts, but the hug feels great.

"You've been working out," Mandy says, eyes wandering over my upper body. "Baggage handling suits you."

The welcome hug done, Cassie folds her arms and fixes me with one of her laser-stares. "Which begs the question, what are you doing turning up on the doorstep, covered in blood?"

"Alright Ally McBeal, let's just say it was unavoidable."

"But Dad, I thought you said— "

"Tell her who your mum is, Ji-min."

"She's my mum."

"Yes, I know that," I say, easing myself off the dining table. "I mean her name."

"Oh, my mum's name is Kim Yunjin."

"Oh," Mandy says, the truth dawning on her.

"That's . . ." Cassie says, as if recalling the story in the papers.

"Yeah," Mandy says.

Cassie puts it together. "So you were . . ."

"Yeah," I say, for once able to take the higher ground. If you can call a revenge killing higher ground.

Ji-min bends down to stroke Mandy's dark-brown cat, Cookie.

"Did you get the guy?" Mandy whispers.

"I got him," I say, keeping my voice down. "Just had to go through some other guys first. And don't two-wrongs me, Cassie."

She shakes her head. "After what I learned on my work placement, maybe the justice system isn't always the answer."

Wow, I'm blown away. My daughter studies law and

loosens up on her morals. Though knowing the lawyers I do, it's probably to be expected.

"God, the poor little thing," Mandy says, looking at Ji-min. "What are we going to do about her?"

"Dunno," I say. "Whatever it is, she can't go into care. You've been there, Mand. You know what it's like."

Mandy nods and tucks her e-cigarette away in a handbag on the kitchen top. "So is this a flying visit or you sticking around for a bit?"

"Why, you sick of me already?" I ask, navigating the wet patches on the kitchen floor, doubtless from where they cleaned up after me.

Mandy shrugs. "Might not be so bad having you round for a while."

"Why, you miss me?"

"Got a few jobs need doing round the house," she adds.

"Ah, now the truth comes out."

"Seriously Dad, you gonna stay around?" Cassie asks, hope in her voice.

"Well, I've been thinking on that," I say, looking at the girls. "Things have changed."

"You mean, career-wise?" Mandy asks.

"No one's chasing my tail anymore," I say. "Might be a good time to return to work."

Cassie takes a breath, about to launch into one. I stop her with a finger. "Let me finish," I say. "This time it'll be on my terms."

"As in?" Cassie asks.

"Think of it like community service," I say. "There are more Yunjins and Ji-mins out there. I've helped a few out on my travels. Maybe it's time I helped a few more out at home. I can do more if I operate from one place. Somewhere I'm known. Somewhere I've got traction."

"Traction?" Cassie says. "You mean threatening people??"

"Steering them round to my way of thinking," I say. "Whenever the ends justify the means."

Cassie huffs and mumbles. "I suppose . . ."

"There's just something I've gotta do first," I say.

"Like what?" Mandy asks. "Something I can do?"

"No, love," I say, flexing my back. "But you could put the kettle on. I could murder a brew."

"I'll make it," Cassie says, the same Marbella tan as her mother. She grabs the kettle and fills it at the tap.

Mandy bends over to where Ji-min kneels with the cat. The kid's got the magic touch. The fucker flies at me all-claws-blazing if I go anywhere near it.

"You want something to eat, sweetheart?" Mandy asks her, her usual hard edges softening out.

Ji-min nods. "Yes please."

"How about fish fingers, chips and beans? Do you eat fish fingers where you're from?"

"She's Korean, Mand. She's not from the bloody moon."

"No swearing around Ji-min," Mandy snaps, pointing an accusing finger.

"Bloody doesn't count," I say, as Mandy cups Ji-min's ears. "And besides, she was born over here."

"Then maybe she'll have a passport," Cassie says, handing me a steaming hot cuppa. "She's still a missing person. It's illegal not to report it."

"Yeah, but this is your father we're talking about," Mandy says, rooting around in a freezer drawer.

"Listen, don't worry about all that," I say. "We'll figure something out." I take a sip of my brew. Cassie offers me the biscuit jar. I look at her funny.

"Blood sugar, Dad. It's what they give you when you donate blood. A tea and a biscuit."

I dig a hand in the jar and demolish one in a single go.

"Just not too many," Mandy says. "I like the trim new Charlie."

Cassie snaps off the end a biscuit with her teeth. "Ugh, I'm gonna vom."

"Why, what's wrong?" I say.

"Sex. You two. The thought of it," Cassie says, pretending to gag.

I laugh. It hurts. I eat another biscuit.

Ji-min looks up at me as she strokes the cat. "Uncle Charlie, what's sex?"

24

I walk through the prison wards, past cell after cell on the top floor of the prison. Some inmates hurl dog's abuse at me. Some lie back on the beds. A few of 'em read. And a few more stare at me like they want to stab me, shoot me or worse.

I scratch my chin where my beard itches. It took me a couple of weeks to grow. But that gave the leg a chance to heal. And the limp to fall away from my stride.

I'm wearing the full screw uniform of white shirt, black trousers and matching knit-jumper with the 'Her Majesty's Prisons' logo on it.

I shake my head at the sight of it. Like it's some kind of regal honour to patrol a shit-hole full of arseholes. Blokes who'd stab your eyes out and steal your fillings given half the chance.

What a royal load of bollocks.

I carry a baton on my right hip. A can of mace on my left. A long chain of keys jangle as I walk, my eyes fixed firm on the end of the walkway.

Dead ahead is the biggest cell in the prison. Two cells

knocked through to form one, all on the say-so of its lone occupant.

I come to a stop outside the cell door. Rudenko sits side on to the door. He's bent over on the edge of his bed, scrolling on an iPad.

He's probably shopping for more goodies for his cell. There's already a TV in front of a leather armchair, while his bed is a double, with a thicker mattress. Plus, he has a table set up with four chairs and deck of cards. And that's not to mention a private sink and a toilet with a wooden seat.

I insert the key in the lock and turn. Roll the door open and step inside.

Rudenko doesn't budge and doesn't even look. "If you're here for my dinner order, I'll have pizza and chips," he says. "And bring me a full bottle of ketchup this time."

I roll the door shut and lock it from the inside. I do it quiet, moving towards the fat Russian.

The backhander was enough for Reg to agree to lend me a uniform and smuggle me in. The beard and disguise enough to get me through the prison corridors unnoticed. But it doesn't fool Rudenko.

"*You,*" he gasps, as he sees me coming.

"Yes, me."

Rudenko puts down the iPad. He rises to his feet. Slow. Wary. "What are you doing here?"

"Did no-one tell you? I work here now."

"*Guard!*" Rudenko yells.

"I'm the only one on duty," I say. "At least on this wing . . . The rest are on a fag break."

"*Guard!*" Rudenko yells again, even louder, backing away from the bed, deeper into his cell.

Which, I might add, makes it easier. Especially since they've walled off the far end of the cell for privacy.

I let the blade slip down from inside my sleeve. A shank with tape around one end, acting as a handle. I catch it in my hand and hold it by my side.

Rudenko holds out his hands. "You want some kind of deal?"

"Your dealing days are over, Ivan," I say, boxing him in. "Mine too."

"Then what do you want from me?" he asks. "Everyone wants something."

"There is something I want," I say. "And you're in the way of it."

Rudenko stands flat against the wall, breathing shallow. Sweating through every hole and pit. "You can't kill me, I'm— "

"You're what? You're no one. Not anymore."

"Come on, Charlie."

"Charlie?" I say. "Who the fuck is Charlie? My name's Breaker."

Rudenko's eyes grow behind his glasses. He knows the game is up. And I let it sink in a minute. Let the thought of it torture him.

Then I do it. Stabbing fast and close. Ten to the heart. Rudenko's whimpers echo off the walls. I let him slide to his fat, hairy arse. He leaves a stripe of blood down the white-painted brick.

He dies fast, his head lolling to one side. Glasses halfway down his nose and his tongue sticking out like a cow with a bolt in its head.

I pull a fistful of tissue off a roll and wrap the shank inside. I drop it in the bog and flush. Moving quick, I clean the blood off my hands in the sink and wipe it down.

I dry off on Rudenko's towel and walk to the door. I

unlock and open. Slide it closed, apply the lock and stride off at pace.

With Rudenko gone and Murphy in the ground, this city might finally have a chance.

People will always want the vices men like Rudenko can provide. But no one has to suffer under the same regime.

I've got an old pal who runs a smaller operation in China Town. He's an entrepreneur at heart. Doesn't get involved in any of the darker sides of the business. No exploitation, abuse, trafficking, prostitution or intimidation.

So maybe he can step into the void. Bring some civility to the streets. Controlled order. Without taking the piss. And if not, if he steps out of line, I'll be there to stop him.

I quicken my step, wanting to clear the prison before the guards return from their team meeting.

I take the central staircase down to ground level, my boots pounding over the metal mesh staircase.

I get halfway down, when I hear the first call.

"Breaker," a voice says from one of the cells.

"Breaker," another calls out.

Another—"Breaker!"

I keep going.

"Break-er, Break-er, Break-er," a man chants slow and steady.

It catches on. At first just a few cells. Then a dozen, fifty, a hundred. The chant sweeps through the entire wing to the point it's deafening.

I stop at the base of the stairs and look around me. In all directions, three floors of inmates reach out from inside their cell doors. They pump their fists and repeat my name.

"Break-er! Break-er! Break-er!"

I look up around the wing, give them a nod and continue on my way.

ALSO BY ROB ASPINALL

CONNECT WITH ROB

Did you enjoy the book?

Rob would love to hear what you think. Please leave an online review wherever's convenient. Your honest feedback will make a huge difference. Thanks for sharing.

Follow Rob:

Instagram: rob_aspinall
Facebook: facebook.com/robaspinallauthor
Twitter: @robaspinall
You can also find Rob on BookBub and Goodreads

robaspinall.com

CPSIA information can be obtained
at www.ICGtesting.com
Printed in the USA
LVHW111505160320
650181LV00002B/720

9 781798 713877